BAILEIGH HIGGINS

From the Ashes

Heroes of the Apocalypse - Book 5

Copyright © 2023 by Baileigh Higgins

All rights reserved. No part of this publication may be reproduced, stored or transmitted in any form or by any means, electronic, mechanical, photocopying, recording, scanning, or otherwise without written permission from the publisher. It is illegal to copy this book, post it to a website, or distribute it by any other means without permission.

This novel is entirely a work of fiction. The names, characters and incidents portrayed in it are the work of the author's imagination. Any resemblance to actual persons, living or dead, events or localities is entirely coincidental.

Baileigh Higgins asserts the moral right to be identified as the author of this work.

Baileigh Higgins has no responsibility for the persistence or accuracy of URLs for external or third-party Internet Websites referred to in this publication and does not guarantee that any content on such Websites is, or will remain, accurate or appropriate.

Designations used by companies to distinguish their products are often claimed as trademarks. All brand names and product names used in this book and on its cover are trade names, service marks, trademarks and registered trademarks of their respective owners. The publishers and the book are not associated with any product or vendor mentioned in this book. None of the companies referenced within the book have endorsed the book.

First edition

This book was professionally typeset on Reedsy. Find out more at reedsy.com

Contents

Acknowledgments	v
Your FREE EBook is waiting!	vi
Dedication	vii
Prologue I - Nikki	1
Prologue II - Lucien	11
Chapter 1 - George	15
Chapter 2 - Mason	21
Chapter 3 - Rocky	30
Chapter 4 - Amelia	34
Chapter 5 - George	41
Chapter 6 - Clare	46
Chapter 7 - Lt. Kingsley	53
Chapter 8 - Theresa	58
Chapter 9 - Nikki	68
Chapter 10 - George	74
Chapter 11 - Amelia	80
Chapter 12 - Bobbi	87
Chapter 13 - George	95
Chapter 14 - Sandi	99
Chapter 15 - Lt. Kingsley	106
Chapter 16 - Priya	111
Chapter 17 - Theresa	116
Chapter 18 - Zoey	122
Chapter 19 - Nikki	129

Chapter 20 - Mason	142
Chapter 21 - Priya	151
Chapter 22 - George	157
Chapter 23 - Clare	161
Chapter 24 - Zoey	166
Epilogue I - Clare	170
Epilogue II - Mason	175
Epilogue III - George	179
Epilogue IV- Nikki	183
Do you want more?	189
Apocalypse Z - Preview	200
Your FREE EBook is waiting!	208
About the Author	209

Acknowledgments

Thank you to Alex for the stunning book cover design. You can find him right here on Facebook for more information: 187 Designz

And a shout-out to all my family, friends, and fans. Without you, I wouldn't be able to live my dream. I appreciate all of your support and kindness.

Your FREE EBook is waiting!

If you'd like to learn more about my books, upcoming projects, new releases, cover reveals, and promotions, simply join my mailing list. Plus, you'll get an exclusive ebook absolutely FREE just for subscribing!

Yes, please. Sign me up!
 https://www.subscribepage.com/i0d7r8

Dedication

This book is dedicated to all the unsung heroes of the world. The men and women who work tirelessly each day to ensure our comfort and safety. Firefighters, paramedics, policemen, doctors, nurses, operators, and more. You are all amazing human beings.

Prologue I - Nikki

Nikki stirred, reluctant to open her eyes. It was much nicer to stay where she was, tucked away in her warm bed. Cooper lay next to her, curled up into a little ball, his chest rising and falling in a comforting rhythm. She snuggled closer to him, pulling the rough blanket up to her nose. Even the hard concrete floor couldn't bother her, the layer of newspapers blocking the worst of the chill.

Gradually, she became aware of a strange sensation. It was alien. So different that it took a while to pinpoint its origin, but she finally found it. A lack of fear. That didn't make any sense, of course. Not with the zombie apocalypse in full swing right outside her door. The monsters were all around, ready to attack at any given moment. She should be scared, but she wasn't. Why?

Then it hit her. Rex was dead. The demon who'd haunted her every waking moment was gone, killed first by the zombie virus, then her. That knowledge took a few minutes to sink into her conscious mind. Her subconscious had realized it long ago, but the rest of her still had to catch up. Amazed by the feeling of lightness in her soul, she sat upright and blinked. "Is this what it feels like to live without terror? To live knowing he's gone?"

Cooper lifted his head and gave her a quizzical look. Nikki laughed and ruffled his fur. "I'm free, Cooper. I'm finally free of that monster, and nothing can ever hurt me again. At least, not like he did."

Cooper's lips pulled back in a smile, and Nikki awarded him with another cuddle. It felt good to be alive. Young, strong, healthy, and free. "Come on, boy. We might as well get up," Nikki said, getting to her feet.

She raised her arms above her head and stretched, her joints popping with the release of tension. A groan escaped her lips, but she froze when an answering groan sounded outside. Dropping into a low crouch, she reached for her bag. Her hand gripped the butt of her gun, and she drew it out without a sound.

Alerted by her sudden change in demeanor, Cooper nudged her hand with his nose and whined. Raising one finger to her lips, Nikki shushed him. In a low whisper, she said, "Quiet, boy. There's something outside. Wait here. Stay."

On silent feet, Nikki moved toward the nearest window. She raised one hand and slowly opened the blinds. A thin stream of grayish light cut through the gloom inside the shop, and she realized it was almost dawn. She'd slept later than expected. Peering through the narrow gap, she looked for the source of the groan she'd heard before.

At first, she saw nothing. The area outside was quiet. Too quiet. Then, a sudden movement drew her attention, and she spotted a figure disappearing around the corner of the building. A flash of stringy dark hair, an awkward shuffle, and a bloodstained shirt were the only things she saw. It was a fleeting glimpse, and she could be wrong, but in her gut, she knew what it was—a zombie.

PROLOGUE I - NIKKI

Cursing under her breath, Nikki sprang into action. There was no time to waste. Once the infected realized she was there, it would attack ruthlessly. With no bars on the windows, it would have no trouble breaking in, and there might be more than one lurking outside. *We'd better get out of here now.*

Closing the gap in the blinds, she ran back toward the bed and gathered her things. She took a brief moment to reassure Cooper, giving the dog a warm hug. "Don't worry, boy. I'll get us out of here, but you must keep quiet."

Cooper's tail wagged. He seemed to understand the need for silence and didn't make a sound while she readied their escape. Throwing her stuff into the backpack, she rolled up her bedding and tied it to the bottom. A bottle of water and a couple of protein bars went into a side pocket in case of an emergency. She'd already packed and loaded the rest of the supplies into the truck the night before, and all she needed to do was get her and Cooper inside its metal embrace before they became zombie food.

She'd slept with her clothes and shoes on, a small blessing Nikki was thankful for now. Securing her belt, she checked the load on both of her guns. The gun she took from Cooper's owner went into her bag as a spare. The other weapon, Rex's old Glock, went into its holster on her belt. With her jacket zipped to her chin and her hair tied into a knot, she was ready to go.

Or almost.

Her stomach churned, and Nikki rolled her eyes. "Damn it. I shouldn't have eaten all that junk last night."

She took Cooper with her to the bathroom and closed the door. The last thing she needed was for the zombies to hear what was about to transpire. The sound effects were sure to be impressive. She felt sorry for Cooper, too. Chips, chocolates, gassy cold drinks, and canned tuna did not go well together.

Afterward, she washed her hands and face, brushed her teeth, and stuffed the remaining toilet roll into her backpack. With Cooper close on her heels, she slipped her pack over her shoulders and prepared to leave.

"Ready, boy?" Cooper dipped his head, looking scared, but he trusted her lead and stuck to her heels.

Gun in hand, Nikki crept toward the door and peered outside. All was quiet, the sun still low on the horizon and the air tinged with gray. Birds chirped in the trees, and a chill breeze rustled through the dried leaves on the ground. There was no sign of the zombie she'd seen earlier, but she was sure it was out there. The creepy boogers had a habit of sneaking up on a person.

Several seconds ticked by while she waited and waited. A mixture of impatience and fear prompted her to make a run for it, but she squashed it down. It wouldn't benefit her to take unnecessary chances. Not while she was still hidden within a reasonably defensible shelter, armed and at full strength. The zombie was out there, and she wanted eyes on it first. It could have friends ready to ambush her at the drop of a hat.

Not for the first time, she realized how fragile life had become. The day before, her seemingly all-powerful stepfather was still alive. Now he was dead, along with countless others much smarter, stronger, and more prepared than she was. The fact that she was still alive boiled down to sheer dumb luck sprinkled with grit and determination. That luck could run out at any moment if she weren't careful, and she could be next on the menu.

"Not today," Nikki said with a determined shake of the head.

"I'm not dying today, and neither is Cooper. Let's find that undead mothersucker before it finds me."

She moved to the next window and peered outside. At first, Nikki saw nothing. As she pulled away, however, a flash of movement caught her eye, and she paused. *What's that?*

A figure lurched into view, one shoulder hanging lower than the other. One foot dragged along the ground, its bare soles torn and bloody. Long dark hair hung past its shoulders, obscuring its face, but it looked like a man. When his head swung toward her, she got a better look and guessed he was in his early twenties. A rocker wearing a torn AC/DC t-shirt and black jeans.

Nikki grinned. "I like the shirt, bro, but what happened to your shoes? One of life's mysteries, huh?"

The disabled zombie shuffled past the window, oblivious to her presence. Its movements were slow and laborious thanks to its crippled state, and it was headed away from the truck. That presented a golden opportunity, and Nikki decided it was now or never. Running from one window to the next, she checked the rest of the perimeter for more undead. When she saw none, her mind was made up. Waving a hand at Cooper, she reached for the door. "Stick close to me, boy."

Cooper whined, his tail tucked between his legs. He didn't look too keen on braving the outside world, and she knew how he felt. "I know, boy. But we can't stay here forever. There's only one of those stinkers out there, and it's a slow one. Let's go."

Twisting the knob, she cracked the door and stuck her head through the gap. The coast was clear, and it was a straight shot to the truck. The doors were unlocked, and the keys were in her pocket. Tightening her hands on the gun, she slipped through the opening and waved to Cooper. He followed her into the open with caution, his head up and his ears pricked for danger.

"Come on, boy," Nikki whispered, dashing toward her vehicle. It was parked behind a couple of trees to keep it hidden from the road. That meant it wasn't as close as she'd have liked, and in her heightened state of anxiety, it felt like miles.

When a howling cry sounded from the left, she knew the zombie had spotted her. It gave chase, but Nikki discounted it as a danger after one swift glance over her shoulder. Its crippled foot rendered it too slow, and it would never catch her at that rate. Grinning, she flashed it the middle finger. "Too slow, dumb ass!"

Suddenly, a chorus of howls rose from a different direction, and Nikki's steps faltered. She searched for the source of the noise and honed in on a clump of bushes not far from her truck. The vegetation crackled as three figures burst into view, hunched over with their hands formed into claws. Their distorted faces were inhuman, and their bloodshot eyes scanned the area for living flesh.

Nikki stared at the trio of monsters, knowing she had but seconds to make it to the truck's safety. These infected were fresh, strong, and agile. Plus, they were fast, driven by hunger and adrenalin. *Can I make it before they do?*

There was no time to debate the question. No point in trying to fight them, either. They'd overwhelm her within seconds. Pushing her body to the limits, she sprinted across the distance, her feet pounding the hard-packed earth. A cloud of dust rose in her wake, churned into the air as her boots dug into the sand. Cooper followed, shadowing her every move.

The infected spotted Nikki and gave chase, howling and

screaming with insane ferocity. They converged on the truck with the kind of speed she couldn't hope to match. The distance closed rapidly, and terror spurted through her veins. *I'm not going to make it!*

Her gaze flashed back and forth between them and the truck, each glance leaching away her courage until she felt exposed. Laid bare to their vicious attack. They were killers; their natures stripped bare of anything but the need to hunt and feed. Distilled to its most basic level, their minds produced no emotion. No sympathy, pain, or fear. She was no match for them, and that knowledge threatened to bring her to her knees.

Nikki slowed, her legs growing heavy with defeat. She raised the gun and braved a couple of shots, but both went wide. The infected never slowed, and they were moments away from cutting off her escape. "I'm not going to make it, boy. You'd better run. They won't go after you while I'm around."

Cooper barked but stuck to her side. A bitter taste stung her mouth when she realized he'd never leave her. He'd stay until the end and die a horrible death, just like her. Regret filled her chest. She'd failed him. She'd failed herself. "I'm sorry, boy."

But Cooper wasn't ready to give up. Not yet. With a wild bark, he dashed ahead, heading straight for the trio of undead. Horror filled her mind as she envisioned her new friend being torn to shreds. "Cooper, no!"

Still barking, Cooper plunged into the infected's midst and rammed into the front runner's legs. It plowed to the ground with an angry snarl, clawing at the earth as it tried to regain its feet. One of its companions raced past and knocked the downed zombie in the face with a wayward knee. Several teeth went flying, and globs of blackened blood flew from its lips.

Down for the count, it flopped around like a fish out of water.

Satisfied with his handiwork, Cooper attacked his next victim, nipping at the infected's heels. The zombie stumbled and slowed, swiping at the furry form that hampered its progress. The dog ran around it in circles, and the infected chased it with arms outstretched. What followed was an awkward dance between the two that would have been funny if it wasn't so dangerous.

Still running, Nikki gaped at the spectacle. Then she realized what Cooper was doing. He was buying her the time she needed to escape. Gratitude filled her heart, and she thanked the stars for his courage and bravery. No matter how scared or terrified, he was still willing to risk his life for hers. "Thank you, Cooper."

Focusing on the truck, she ran as fast as she could. It would be a crime to waste the precious time bought by Cooper's selfless act, and she needed to make the most of it. Besides, he needed her help too, and she was the only one able to give it. Through gritted teeth, she said, "Don't worry, boy. I've got you."

Seconds later, she slid to a halt next to the truck. A glance showed her that the crippled zombie was still a safe distance away, and she turned her attention back to Cooper and the trio of fresh zombies. Zom number one was on its knees, picking itself up from the dirt. Zom number two was still busy running in circles like a clown, but Zom number three was almost upon her. So fast that she barely had time to aim her gun.

The first shot went wild, zooming off into the distance, and Nikki cursed. "Too fast!"

Steadying her pose, she blew out a breath and tried again. Bang!

PROLOGUE I - NIKKI

This time, the bullet grazed the zombie's shoulder. It snarled and kept coming, even faster than before, and liquid terror spurted through Nikki's veins. *Come on, come on! You can do this!*

The third shot hit it in the chest, and the zombie faltered.

A fourth shot pulverized the jaw, and the lower half of its face disintegrated. A mess of black blood, ruined muscles, tendons, and crushed bone dangled down its chest, and its tongue lolled from the gaping hole like a gray worm. It was enough to make Nikki lose her lunch, but there was no time to be squeamish. Cooper depended on her. "Focus, Nikki. Focus!"

The fifth shot entered the forehead and exploded out of the back of the skull in a mass of pink brain matter and glistening bone. The zombie jerked to a step and fell backward, its undead life cut short.

Almost crying with relief, Nikki yanked open the truck door and yelled, "Cooper, get in!"

Cooper barked in answer and abandoned his zombie playmate. Streaking across the earth like a golden comet, he reached her side within seconds and flew into the cab. Sliding across the smooth leather seat, his nails scrabbling for purchase, he barked at her to get in. "Woof, woof!"

"Good boy," Nikki cried, jumping behind the wheel. She slammed the door shut, locked it, and reached for the keys. A split-second later, the first zombie slammed into the vehicle, followed by the second, who'd finally found its feet, and the crippled zombie, lagging way behind the rest.

Growling with hunger, they clawed at the glass, their undead faces filled with creepy yearning. Nikki shuddered and twisted the key in the ignition. "Not today, suckers."

With a roar of the engine, she sped away, leaving a cloud

of dust and three frustrated zombies in her wake. They gave chase but were soon lost in the distance, becoming nothing more than a bad memory.

Heaving a sigh, Nikki settled back into her seat and reached for Cooper. Giving him a rub, she said, "Thanks, boy. Once again, you saved my bacon. I owe you one."

Cooper licked her hand and lay down on the seat, his head resting next to her thigh. Filled with warmth and gratitude, Nikki looked to the road ahead, wondering what more lay in store for them. One thing she knew for a fact. *I'm not alone anymore. With Cooper by my side, I can face anything.*

Prologue II - Lucien

Once they'd accomplished their mission, Lucien and his two teammates abandoned the hospital to its fate and ran across the grounds toward the walls. They hunkered down behind a clump of bushes and waited until the coast was clear. It wasn't long before the first sounds of their handiwork reached them.

First, there was a deathly hush. Almost as if the night held its collective breath while it waited for chaos to descend on the quiet scene. Then came the sound of commands shouted in the distance, followed by the first scattered cries from within the building. The cries soon turned into screams, and the grounds exploded into action as the guards realized what was happening.

Shouts, curses, and conflicting orders rang out, and emergency spotlights flooded the area with light. The muffled pops of scattered gunshots reached Lucien's ears, underlaid by the muted din inside the building. Vehicles rumbled to life as the guards prepared for a mass evacuation.

Lucien listened to it all with a smile playing on his lips. He doubted there would be many survivors. The attack was too sudden, and the odds were against the people trapped inside the hospital. In the morning, there would be no one left to call it home anymore. Only the undead and they didn't care about anything except their need to feed.

Blackwell, Lucien, and the rest of their team would sweep in, lure away the zombies, and take what they wanted from the remains. Like vultures picking over a carcass. It was a simple strategy that worked every time.

As for the people who died, they were nothing more than a means to an end. While Lucien harbored no ill will toward them, he felt no sympathy for them either. It was the apocalypse, and civilized society and its rules no longer existed. Only the strong deserved to survive, while the weak needed to die. It was logical and the way nature intended. Once the zombies were gone, only the strongest of humanity would remain, ready to inherit the earth. *And I plan to be one of them.*

Sudden footsteps alerted him to company, and he hunched down lower behind the bush. The steps came closer and closer, and he identified two pairs of treads. Guards, most likely. *Shit! We were almost in the clear.*

He glanced at his companions and removed the knife from its sheath on his belt. Placing one finger on his lips, he nodded. A silent command. They nodded back, their knives held ready in their hands. Together, they waited in tense readiness.

Two figures ran around the corner of the wall, straight into Lucien's group. Their eyes widened, and they stumbled to a halt, their hands going to their guns.

Lucien launched himself through the air, his knife flashing silver in the light. The blade cut through the tender flesh of his chosen victim's throat. It sliced through muscle and tendon, severing the artery. Crimson fluid spurted from the gash, and the man gurgled as he went down with Lucien on top of him.

Lucien held the man down, his hands growing slick with blood. Baring his teeth, he growled, "Die."

PROLOGUE II - LUCIEN

The man gasped, blood bubbling from his lips. He swatted at Lucien, but his hands held no strength. He was already dead. He just didn't know it yet. When his eyes glazed over and his body stilled, Lucien let go and jumped to his feet. The other guard was also down, and he nodded with satisfaction. Wiping his bloody hands clean on his shirt, he said, "Check the wall."

"The coast is clear," one of his teammates said after taking a quick look.

Lucien nodded. "Good. Let's go before more come."

As one, they scaled the wall and dropped to the other side. They sprinted down the road, heading for their headquarters. They moved fast and kept their eyes peeled for more undead as they ran. Rotters would be drawn from all over town by the noise and commotion, an unfortunate by-product of their endeavors.

It didn't matter, however. Blackwell would be pleased with their work. The hospital was their biggest target yet and contained enough supplies to carry them for months. They could live off its stores in comfort and without risking their lives.

It was not a sustainable way of living. That much, Lucien realized. Eventually, they'd run out of targets to hit. Survivors would become scarce with time, as would supplies. There was only so much to go around, after all.

When that day came, they'd have to evolve. They'd have to settle down and form a community of their own. A place that was safe from the zombies and could provide for their needs: Food, water, shelter, medicine, weapons, and more.

Such a place didn't need a government, police, army, laws, or democracy. It only required an overlord and his henchmen. A strong and ruthless leader capable of making the hard decisions. The remaining survivors would be little more than servants—enslaved people who labored for their master. In return, they'd be kept safe from the zombies, if not their human overlord and his crew.

It wasn't fair, but nothing in the world was fair. Lucien had learned that lesson early in his life. When Blackwell became the king of his domain, Lucien would be right there standing next to him. His second-in-command and trusted advisor. *I will not labor under the boot of a tyrant. Instead, I will be a tyrant.*

Chapter 1 - George

Miles away, while Nikki still lay sleeping, George tossed and turned in his bed. The stump at the end of his arm itched and burned, making it impossible to sleep. Sometimes, it felt like his arm was still there, just out of sight and touch. A phenomenon called phantom limb syndrome. According to Dr. Bond, it was expected, a result of a mix-up between signals in the nervous system, specifically between the spinal cord and brain. However, knowing it was normal didn't relieve the discomfort, and medication had little effect.

Finally, George got tired and threw aside his blankets. On tiptoe, he crept toward the exit, careful not to make a sound. On either side, his friends and colleagues lay snoring in their beds, exhausted after the long day. The last thing he wanted to do, was to wake anyone up. Nobody needed to hear about his problems, trivial as they were.

Slipping into the dim hallway, he looked to the left and right before heading toward the men's bathroom. The corridors were empty at that time of the night, and most of the residents were fast asleep in their beds. Guards patrolled the walls outside, keeping the slumbering community safe from the infected wandering the streets of Burlington.

George scratched at the stump where his arm used to be and

frowned with envy. The guards were lucky. They possessed all of their limbs and were allowed to carry guns, leave the grounds on supply runs, shoot zombies, defend their families, and live on the edge. It was an exhilarating existence, similar to being a firefighter. It was also the kind of life that was now out of reach for him, cut away along with his diseased limb.

With a sigh, he made his way through the empty, echoing hallways toward the men's bathrooms. He pushed the door open, and it swung inward on creaky hinges. Inside, the room was empty, lit by a single flickering lightbulb, and the tiles gleamed with a sterile glow. The smell of antiseptic made his nose twitch and his eyes water. It was a smell he'd come to hate since the amputation.

After emptying his full bladder, he washed his single hand. His movements were awkward, and he fumbled with the soap. It would take time to train his left hand to do the right hand's job and even longer to get used to the missing part of his body. Everything was a struggle, and he realized how much he'd taken for granted. *I should've been more grateful for what I had instead of constantly complaining.*

Staring at his reflection in the mirror, he found it hard to believe that the thin, gaunt-eyed man staring back at him was himself. He looked older, and he'd lost weight since his near brush with death. His eyes were sunk deep into the hollows of his skull, and his cheekbones were sharp and bony. A grayish tint had replaced his former tan, sucking the life from his complexion. "I look like a damn zombie. Hell, I might as well be one."

It'd been a narrow escape, after all. By rights, he should be moldering in a mass grave with a bullet hole in his forehead, put there by Robert or one of the other firefighters. Instead,

CHAPTER 1 - GEORGE

he was still alive. Crippled but breathing. He could only hope that he'd adjust in time. That he could learn to be a valuable part of the community once more instead of a burden. *I don't want to be a parasite. I want to help. I want to be a fighter again—a hero.*

The thought that he might never regain his former stature was disheartening, and George splashed water on his face. The cool liquid relieved his anxiety, and he ducked his head under the running water. Moments later, he heard muffled cries and came up for air in a rush. The sounds were distant but urgent, possibly even scared, and he paused to listen. Water ran from the tap unheeded, swirling down the drain, but he hardly noticed the wastage. When the cries turned into screams, he knew there was trouble inside the hospital. Big trouble. *Zombies!*

Closing the tap, George ran toward the door and pushed it open. A symphony of growls and snarls, punctuated by gunshots, assaulted his ears. A couple of people ran past, too panicked to notice his presence in the open doorway. He reached out to the nearest one and yelled, "Hey, stop! What's going on?"

The woman ignored him and kept running, disappearing around a corner. Several more people streamed past while George hesitated, unsure what to do. Should he follow them? Run? Look for help? Answers?

Before he could decide, a guy wearing a blood-stained t-shirt stumbled into him. George stepped backward, and the man collapsed to the floor, sobbing. "Help me, please. Help!"

George bent down to help but paused when he saw the vicious bite marks on the man's face, neck, and collarbone. "Oh, shit. What happened to you?"

"The dead. They're inside," the man said, his breathing harsh and labored.

"How?" George cried, horrified.

"I… I don't know, they… they're everywhere," the man said, slumping to the floor. A pool of blood crept across the tiles, and his eyes grew dim. A rattling cough signaled his death, and the stranger grew still.

George stared at the body for a few seconds, processing the information he'd received. It was simple. The undead were inside the building, killing and infecting its unsuspecting inhabitants. He had to warn his people, but how? Unarmed except for his ax, he couldn't take on a mob of zombies. That was suicide. *But I can save Amelia. She's stuck in the psych ward, not far from here. If I hurry, I can make it.*

***

Deep within the hospital, hundreds of zombies flooded the ground floor of the building. Oblivious to the danger, the community slept, tucked away in their warm beds, unaware of the tramping feet headed their way—a veritable march of the undead.

Ravenous.

Relentless.

Unstoppable.

The smell of rot preceded them. A stench that tainted everything in its path. For weeks, they'd moldered within the confines of the morgue, trapped inside its walls and their decomposing bodies. Veins ruptured, bowels emptied, bladders spilled, and muscles decayed. Tendons stiffened, blood pooled and dried, and skin rotted. Now, they were free, but they were still prisoners of the flesh, caught within the morbid remains of their corpses.

CHAPTER 1 - GEORGE

One of the front runners, a young male nurse, shuffled forward as fast as his weakened limbs allowed. The tag on his uniform read Anzo, the name he used to bear in life. A name he'd been proud of once. It was strange. A little exotic. Chosen by a mother who liked fantasy books more than she wanted real life. Girls liked it too, and it got him a lot of attention. Now it mattered nothing.

Fit and healthy in life, he'd decayed slower than some of his brethren and was able to push to the front. His basic instincts told him that was where the action would be. At the head of the pack, first to the scene of the kill. He didn't reason this out in his mind. He wasn't able to think at all, but somehow he knew there'd be no food at the back, lost within the mob of undead.

With a snarl, Anzo shoved aside a woman who blocked his way. She stumbled to the side and knocked into a wooden barrier. The barrier gave way, swinging open to reveal a darkened interior filled with warmth and life. A wash of air from within tickled his nostrils, and he smelled the delectable scent of living flesh tinged with blood. It was faint, but it was there, and he immediately changed course and headed inside the opening. The female zombie followed, also drawn by the promise of food. Together, they shuffled toward a row of objects filled with humanoid lumps.

Anzo reached out with cold fingers and grasped something warm. It wiggled beneath his touch, and he strengthened his grip. The wriggly thing tried to pull away, and he knew it was alive. A spurt of something akin to excitement flushed through his mind, and he pounced on the warm, wriggling thing. Though it wasn't an emotion, it promised fulfillment. A cessation of the hunger that gnawed at his innards like a rat. If he could think and feel, he would've marveled at the sheer complexity of a virus that could take control of the human brain and cause it to crave living flesh. All in a bid to spread and propagate the disease

The thing beneath him screamed with terror. Spurred on by his victim's cries, Anzo sank his teeth into its delicious flesh. Blood flooded his mouth, and he tore a strip of meat free from the bone. It flapped around while he chewed, blood coating his hands and face. It felt like bathing in the essence of life, and he dove back in for more.

Other zombies joined him, and the ward turned into a bloodbath. Deprived for weeks, they feasted like rabid wolves, pouncing on one victim after another. Many of their prey got away with their lives, though injured. It was the way of the virus. Infected, they'd return to their own to turn later and infect more healthy hosts. Others died and turned on the spot, swelling the numbers of the horde. Bathed in blood, Anzo and his brethren heralded the fall of the Virtua Willingboro Hospital.

Chapter 2 - Mason

When Mason and Kingsley realized the hospital was overrun, they sprang into action. Kingsley pulled his sidearm from its holster and handed it to Mason. "Sound the alarm. Get as many of our people out as you can."

"Where are you going?" Mason asked.

"Calling the guards. It's all hands on deck now," Lieutenant Kingsley said, "Plus, I need to open the armory. Meet you there."

"Stay safe," Mason said, watching as Kingsley ducked through the exit. Turning back, he gripped the gun in his right hand, locked and loaded. He carried his fire ax in his left hand, ready to fight. The groans of the undead were louder now, and the smell of rot clung to the roof of his mouth. *I'd better hurry. They're moving fast. Way too fast.*

With single-minded determination, Mason plunged into the depths of the hospital. Setting a course for his ward, he ran as fast as his legs could carry him. Bellowing at the top of his lungs, he tried to warn the other inhabitants of danger. "Code Red. Code Red. The hospital is overrun. Evacuate. Evacuate!"

As he sprinted through the halls, pale and frightened faces appeared in his wake, popping up in open doorways. Scattered cries followed him, asking desperate questions, but he refused to stop and answer. There was no time. He had to get to his people. He had to get to Clare. Instead, he repeated his warning. "Evacuate. Evacuate!"

Outside, alarms began to blare, adding their strident wail to the mix. They did more to warn the inhabitants than Mason ever could, and people burst from every possible nook and cranny.

They streamed through the hallways, screaming and crying. Some carried babies, others dragged children by the hand, while still others pushed relatives in wheelchairs. It was a chaotic scene, and the press of bodies soon slowed his progress. Cursing, he ducked into a side corridor where it was quieter. It led away from the main entrance and toward the trauma bay, where incoming personnel were checked for bites and quarantined. At night, it was generally peaceful, and he hoped he'd be able to get back to his people before the zombies got there.

However, Mason hadn't gone far when a woman charged out of a nearby room and grabbed his arm. He tried to pull free, not wanting to stop, but she had him in a death grip, hanging on with both arms.

"What's going on?" she cried, her eyes wild.

"Infected. They're inside the hospital," Mason replied, prying her fingers loose from his arm.

The woman gasped. "What? Where? How?"

"I don't have time for this," Mason said, backpedaling.

"Please, you have to help me," she begged.

"I can't. I have to warn the others," Mason said, growing desperate.

Suddenly, a second figure emerged from the doorway behind the woman, looming above them like a mountain. "Beatrice.

CHAPTER 2 - MASON

Let go of him. He can't help you."

"But… the dead are inside the hospital, Rocky. What do we do?" the woman wailed, visibly shaking.

"Rocky?" Mason repeated with a frown. He stepped closer, recognizing the man as one of the orderlies in the quarantine ward. "Are there patients in there? Amelia? George?"

"It's just the woman now. Amelia," Rocky replied.

"Shit, we have to get her out," Mason said.

"I'll do it," Rocky said. "You warn the rest."

"Are you sure?" Mason asked, hesitating. As much as he wanted to get to Clare and the others, Amelia was also his family. Robert's wife. He had to make sure she was alright.

Rocky nodded. "Do what you have to do. I'll get Beatrice and Amelia to safety, I promise."

"Thanks," Mason said, relieved.

Not wasting any more time, he dashed down the hall and resumed his earlier warnings. "Code Red. Code Red. The hospital is overrun. Evacuate. Evacuate!"

"Evacuate?"

"What?" a woman cried.

"Just get the hell out of here, Ma'am," Mason answered, not slowing down. He ducked around a few more stragglers, people drifting around looking for answers that would never come.

The volume of screams kept growing louder as the infected invaded the quarters of the living. The smell of undead flesh and decay crept through the corridors like a haze of death, underlaid by the coppery tinge of blood, and Mason prayed he wasn't too late. It was just a little farther. Right around the…

Mason slid around the corner, arms windmilling for balance, and slammed into a wall of bodies. Dead bodies.

As one, the mob of infected turned to face him, eager for the fresh meat that had stumbled into their midst. The stench of rot enfolded him. Hooked fingers grabbed for his hair, clothes, and skin. Cold hands gripped his arms, and rotten teeth moved in for the kill.

Bang!

Bang!

Bang, bang!

Gunshots perforated the chorus of hungry growls, and several zombies tumbled to the ground. Confused, the rest twisted and turned, searching for the source of the noise. Those that fell were trampled to death, bones crushed, and skulls broken by careless feet.

Mason took his chance and flopped to the ground, breaking free from the hands that sought to rip him apart. Rolling backward, he reached the open and jumped to his feet. A couple of calculated hacks with his ax cleared away the nearest infected, and he gained a precious few seconds to catch his breath.

Before he could move, wild yells broke loose from a nearby wing, and a set of double doors slammed open. People streamed from the interior, wielding an assortment of weapons: Guns, bats, pipes, shower rails, knives, axes, and even an umbrella. The crowd exploded into the midst of the zombie mob with killer rage, and the ranks of the undead quickly thinned beneath the onslaught.

Yelling and waving his ax, Mason joined the fight, hacking and slashing his way across the hallway. A backward blow sent one infected tumbling to the ground. It tripped several of its rotter friends, and he quickly dispatched the lot with quick strikes to their skulls.

CHAPTER 2 - MASON

Stepping over the pile of arms, limbs, and torsos, he hit another one in the temple, reversed the blow, and sent a second flying into the ground. A crawler grabbed his leg, teeth bared and ready to sink into his shin.

With a grimace of disgust, Mason kicked it in the face. A quick shot punched through its brain, and it slumped to the ground.

A look showed him that he was halfway across the hall, closing in on the other survivors battling the horde. This gave him renewed hope, and he attacked a knot of zombies with fresh vigor.

When a flash of orange caught his eye, an involuntary smile wreathed his face, and joy rose in his chest. *A fireman's jacket!*

The people fighting for their lives mere yards away were his people. He'd made it to them in time. Maybe not to warn them, but to help them. Standing on tiptoe, he waved his ax and yelled over the heads of the zombies, "Clare? Are you there?"

"Bro? Is that you?" came the answer.

"Over here," Mason yelled, waving the ax some more. Then the zombies closed in again, and he had to back away.

A few more shots rang out, but the shooters hung back, unwilling to let loose in the crowded area. It would be too easy to hit one of their own, and he applauded their caution.

Bit by bit, he fought his way toward the oasis of humanity across the hall. One by one, the divide of infected grew smaller until finally, he came face to face with a familiar grin. Relief flooded his veins. "Clare. You're safe."

"Of course I am," Clare replied, cocky as ever.

"Mason! Thank God," another voice called out, and he spotted Theresa at the back, wielding a gun. Several more cries of relief greeted his arrival, but there was no time to stop and exchange pleasantries. Zombies pressed in from every side, eager for their pound of flesh.

Moving to her side, Mason joined up with Clare. Together with the rest of the team, they advanced on the infected and thinned their ranks. More zombies fell with every hack, slash, blow, and chop. Gobs of blackened blood, rotten brains, and slimy entrails coated the floor, and a carpet of bodies formed underfoot.

Mason stepped in a pool of gore and slipped, nearly going down, but a firm hand grabbed his elbow. He looked up into the grim face of Frank. The ex-cop helped him back to his feet, gave a curt nod, and said, "Careful now. You just made it back to us."

"Uh-huh," Mason said, sucking in a huge gulp of air. "Thanks."

"Watch out," Frank said, pushing him out of the way. A straggler snarled at them, but a quick bullet from Frank's gun pulverized the zombie's brain, and it collapsed like a sack of rotten meat.

A few more infected followed, picked off by the firefighters until the last one died a gruesome but final death. Silence fell over the corridor, broken only by everyone's harsh breathing. Killing infected was no easy job. It required a massive amount of stamina to keep fighting. To keep lifting one's arm long after it grew numb. It was why they all trained every day—a fact Mason was now very grateful for.

Rolling his aching shoulders, he tucked Kingsley's gun into his belt and wiped the blade of his ax on the shirt of the nearest dead zombie. Next, he surveyed Clare with a critical eye. "Are you okay? No bites? Scratches?"

CHAPTER 2 - MASON

"I think I'm good," Clare said, blood speckling her fair skin. Stringy dark hair surrounded her face, and she wore a rumpled t-shirt, baggy tracksuit pants, and socks soaked in blood and offal.

"You think?" he said with a frown.

"I'm fine. Promise," Clare said with a groan. "Just… where did they come from? What happened?"

"Yes, do you know what's going on?" Theresa asked, pushing to the front of the group.

"The dead inside the morgue got out. At least, that's what I think," Mason said.

"My God," Theresa whispered, her cheeks turning pale. "They're inside?"

"They're everywhere," Mason confirmed. "This must've been a splinter group."

"What about everyone else?" Theresa asked. "Did they get out?"

"I don't know. I doubt it. Lieutenant Kingsley sounded the alarm, and I tried to warn everyone, but…." Mason trailed off, unwilling to finish the sentence.

In the distance, a medley of screams, gunshots, and blaring alarms told its own story, and Theresa shook her head. "We have to help where we can. Save as many as possible."

"Yes, but we can't help anyone if we're dead," Frank pointed out. "If the hospital is overrun, we must get everyone to safety first. After that, those who can fight should head to the armory. Only then can we hope to help anyone."

Mason nodded. "Frank's right. We can't fight them like this. We need guns. Kingsley said he'd open the armory. We just have to get there."

"Okay, so that's the plan," Theresa said, looking around. "Is everyone here? Everyone accounted for?"

"Sandi, Claudia, the other teachers, parents, and kids, including Paisley, sleep in a separate ward next to the schoolroom," Clare pointed out.

"We'll have to come back for them," Mason said. "That part of the hospital is overrun."

"We'd better hurry," Clare said. "Leo and Sarah are on guard duty. They should be outside."

"George is missing," Bobbi said, raising one hand.

"Damn. Does anyone know where he is?" Theresa asked.

"No, but if he hears the alarms, he'll try to save Amelia. She's locked up in the psych ward," Bobbi said.

"Don't worry. She's safe. Rocky, the caretaker, promised he'd get her out," Mason said. "I met him on the way here."

"George doesn't know that," Bobbi said, a flash of worry crossing her face. "I'll find him and meet you outside in the parking lot. We'll need vehicles to get everyone out."

"Wait, it's too dangerous," Theresa cried.

"I'll be fine," Bobbi said. She walked over and shoved something into Theresa's arms. "Take care of Sebastian."

"Okay," Theresa said, hugging the crate to her chest.

"Thanks," Bobbi said before dashing off.

Mason watched her leave with a frown. "She's right about needing vehicles. Those who can't fight should head to the safe house."

"Alright," Frank said. "Let's go. Lead the way, Mason."

"Yes, Sir," Mason affirmed, gripping his ax with a sweaty palm.

Turning back the way he'd come, he headed for the ER exit. It was the closest and a straight shot to the parking lot. The rest of the group followed him through the twists and turns of the hospital, a tight-knit group of survivors. Looking at their determined expressions, he realized once again how lucky he was to end up with people of their caliber. Together, they could handle anything that came their way.

Chapter 3 - Rocky

The moment Mason left, Rocky considered the best way to get himself, Beatrice, and Amelia to safety. He was responsible for them. A responsibility he took very seriously. For that reason, he always ensured he was on hand whenever new patients were booked in or when a particularly volatile patient interacted with Dr. Kent Bond or one of the nurses. It was also the reason he stood watch at night, relieved in the early morning hours by a volunteer from Lieutenant Kingsley's guard.

Now, he faced a problem. On the one hand, he had to get Beatrice somewhere safe. But he also had to get Amelia out of her room and back to her people if possible. Thankfully, she was the only patient in residence that day. That still left him with Beatrice, and she looked ready to stroke out at any moment.

"Beatrice, look at me. We have to save Amelia. She's locked inside her room, and we have to get her out of there," Rocky said.

"What? No, there's no time!" Beatrice cried out. "We need to run! Run!"

"Beatrice, please. We can't abandon our patient," Rocky added, placing one steadying hand on Beatrice's shoulder.

"She'll be fine. She's locked in, and nothing can get to her,"

Beatrice said, wringing her hands. "Please, let's go. Please."

"You'd leave her to starve to death?" Rocky asked, unable to believe his ears. While they'd never been friends, he'd always respected Beatrice for her efficiency and professionalism. He'd never have thought her capable of such selfishness.

"Someone will find her. Her people will come looking for her," Beatrice said, shaking her head. Tears poured down the woman's face, and her body shook like a leaf in the wind.

Rocky stared at his colleague, trying to form a plan. It was clear Beatrice was in full-blown panic mode and not about to go back for Amelia, but he couldn't leave an innocent woman locked up to die. The screams, gunshots, groans, howls, and alarms formed a distant din, but it was growing louder with each passing second. It pressed in around them, adding to Rocky's sense of urgency. Whatever he was going to do, it had to be soon. By the sound of things, the infected were getting close. Too close.

"Wait here. I'll fetch Amelia," Rocky said, turning toward the psych ward.

"No, I can't," Beatrice wailed.

"Just wait. I won't be long," Rocky insisted.

"No, I'm leaving. You can stay if you want," Beatrice cried before breaking into a run. She dashed down the corridor, but she took the wrong turn in her headlong flight. Instead of making for the ER exit, she headed deeper into the hospital. Straight toward the undead.

"Beatrice, no!" Rocky yelled, his voice booming throughout the space. "Come back!"

Beatrice cast one last look at him, her cheeks wet with tears and her eyes wild, but she didn't stop. Instead, she disappeared around a corner, lost from sight.

"Damn you, woman!" Rocky bellowed, his frustration turning into anger. Sprinting down the corridor, Rocky tried to catch up to the fleeing Beatrice. As he drew closer, he heard her sudden shrill screams, and his stomach dropped to the floor. Rounding the corner, he slid to a stop, shock and horror fizzing through his veins.

A wall of death filled the hallway, and dozens of hungry faces turned toward him, ready to devour his flesh. Backpedaling, he scrambled to put distance between himself and the infected, retreating back the way he came.

Beatrice was not so lucky. She hadn't noticed the zombies in her panicked state until it was too late. Hands, fingers, and teeth reached out to grab her, pulling them into their midst. Blood fountained from dozens of wounds as the mob swarmed over her body. Her clothes were torn from her body, her flesh ripped apart, and her innards pulled from the open crater her stomach had become. Her agonized screams turned to gurgles and, finally, to silence as she mercifully blacked out.

Mere feet away, Rocky stared at the scene with revulsion and pity. The person he'd once known as a colleague and fellow human being was now nothing more than a pile of meat feeding a rabid mob of cannibals.

Suddenly, a figure lunged at him from the shadows. Clawed hands gripped his collar, and glistening teeth sank into his throat. Gnawing, gnashing, and chewing, the sharp canines tore through the artery and windpipe. Warm blood gushed from the wound and flooded his lungs.

Choking and gasping for air, Rocky had just enough strength left to club his attacker in the head with one meaty fist. The infected fell away, and he half-ran, half-staggered back the way he'd come. Like a blind man, he sought safety and refuge. The only place that could offer that was the psych ward, and he headed toward it, but each step was slower than the last. His limbs grew heavy, and his sight dimmed. Denied life-giving oxygen and blood, his brain starved, and his organs failed.

Six feet from the doors of the psych ward, Rocky fell to the floor and breathed his last, but inside his blood, the virus was already at work. Taking swift control of his nervous system, it began the process of reanimation. Dead no more, Rocky was reborn.

Chapter 4 - Amelia

Amelia listened to the alarms blaring throughout the compound, her mind racing as she considered her options. She didn't have many. As a patient with mental instability, she was locked into her room at night. Nor was she allowed anything resembling a weapon. Even her outfit was no defense against the undead, consisting of cotton underwear, a pale blue shirt, matching pants, and bare feet. *Think, think, think!*

Rushing toward her bed, she ripped the sheet from the mattress and used her teeth to tear it into long strips. It wasn't easy, but the material was old and worn by frequent washing. Soon, she had an armful of linen strips. Working fast, she wound the ribbons around her hands and forearms, creating a thick material barrier between her flesh and the gnashing teeth of zombies. She did the same to her feet, ankles, and shins, feeling a little like a ninja by the time she was done.

Next, she flipped the bed onto its side and freed one of the metal legs from the socket. She'd long since used a butterknife to remove the screws keeping it in place, and it slid free without any trouble. Armed with the metal pipe, she charged the door and smashed through the small observation window set inside the frame.

The chaos inside the hospital drowned out the sound of

CHAPTER 4 - AMELIA

shattering glass, and she cleared away the jagged edges with the pipe. As soon as the window was out, she reached through the opening and unlatched the door from the outside. It clicked open without a hitch, and she slammed it against the wall in her haste to escape. Outside her room, the corridor was bare. Not a soul could be seen, which she found surprising. Usually, either Rocky or Beatrice manned the cubicle at the far end, ever watchful of the patients under their care.

"Hello? Anyone there?" Amelia cried, but nobody answered. "Huh. They must've gone to investigate the alarm."

Grabbing the opportunity, Amelia sprinted toward the far end of the hallway. The door was unlocked, and she cracked it open to get a better look at the common room beyond. The space was empty, and the nurse's station was deserted. A couple of lights shone overhead, and a chair lay on its side, which pointed to a possible panic. That caused her to frown. *Did they hear the sirens and run? Rocky? Beatrice? Even Daisy? Did they abandon me? Leave me to die?*

It was hard to believe, but the evidence was right in front of her face. Whoever was on shift that night, they'd run at the first sign of trouble, leaving her alone and defenseless—locked inside her room. Anger flashed through her veins. "Assholes!"

She jogged toward the nurse's station at the far end and ducked behind it, searching for anything useful. There was little but a stack of papers, books, stationary, a now-defunct computer, a telephone, and a bottle of water. "Shit!"

Cursing, Amelia sprinted toward the exit, having no choice but to face the unknown in her pajamas. She ran through the door and found herself on the edge of a screaming crowd of panicking people. They streamed toward the hospital's exit en masse, their cries creating a deafening din.

After weeks of solitude, the sheer crush of bodies and sound was overwhelming, and Amelia ran back the way she came, slamming the door shut behind her. Her heart raced within her chest, threatening to break through the cage of bone that kept it prisoner. Her breath sawed in and out of her lungs, and black encroached on her vision.

"You've got to be kidding me! I'm going to faint?" Amelia cried, pressing one hand to her heaving chest. On wobbly legs, she stumbled toward the nurse's station and grabbed the water bottle. Removing the cap, she took a couple of gulps before splashing the rest of the liquid onto her face. The action revived her, and her mind cleared. "Come on, Amelia. Get your shit together. You can do this."

Gathering her courage, she ran back to the door, ready to face the crowd. This time, she kept a tight rein on her fear using a technique Robert once taught her a long time ago. She was due to speak at a business conference, and her nerves got the better of her. When it was time for her to go onstage, she panicked and froze on the spot. But Robert was there, talking her through it.

"Breathe, darling. In and out. In and out," Robert said, gripping her shoulders. "Remember. They're just people like you and me. Nothing more. Nothing special."

"O... okay," Amelia said, nodding.

"Now breathe. In and out. Focus on that. Focus on taking deep, steady breaths while you talk. Feel the air flowing in and out of your lungs. Fresh, life-giving air. Okay?" Robert said, his expression earnest. "You can do this."

"Yes, I can do this," Amelia said, feeling much calmer.

"That's it," Robert said with a smile. "Now knock 'em dead."

The memory reminded her of him, and she could almost

CHAPTER 4 - AMELIA

hear his calm, steady voice in her ears. He would want her to be brave. He would want her to escape. To live. He would not want her to die because she was too scared to do anything and chose to hide like a frightened rabbit.

"Alright, Robert. This is me being brave," Amelia said, yanking the door wide open.

A zombie filled the frame, looming large in the shadows. A deep growl rumbled through its chest. A monster. The stuff of nightmares.

Amelia screamed and stumbled backward, raising her weapon to fend off the monstrosity. With a howl, it attacked, arms as thick as treetrunks ready to rip her into a thousand bloody chunks. Amelia swung the pipe at its head, and it connected with a hollow thunk. The metal vibrated from the impact, shattering her grip, and she dropped the pipe with a pained cry. Unfazed, the infected kept coming, his massive bulk charging toward her like a freight train.

Cradling her wrists, Amelia ducked beneath its outstretched arms and scrambled to the side, seeking a way around the massive zombie. A chair blocked her way, and she had to dance backward to stay out of reach as the infected grabbed for her again. Though big, the monster was surprisingly fast, and it was all she could do to keep herself out of its deadly grip. Unable to fight, her only hope was to escape if she could make it to the exit.

The infected swiped at her with a thunderous roar, and she ducked, but she was too slow this time. Its fist connected with her jaw, and white-hot pain exploded through her brain. Shocked and in agony, she flew through the air, hitting the ground with terrific force. A pained grunt escaped her lips as she tried to find her feet, knowing she had mere seconds before he was on her once again.

A shadow fell across her form, and terror spurted through her veins. Through tear-filled eyes, she glanced up at her attacker. Illuminated by one of the fluorescent ceiling lights, she caught a glimpse of his face, and recognition shot through her mind. *Rocky!*

First, her caretaker, and now, her killer, he towered above her like an unstoppable force. Despair weighed Amelia down, knowing she was outmatched. As good as dead. She could prolong the inevitable, or she could give in with grace. She closed her eyes and waited for him to reach down and grab her. She imagined brute hands picking her up before vicious teeth tore out her throat. Hopefully, her death would be quick.

Suddenly, a crack filled the air, and her eyes popped open. Looking up, she stared at the gaping hole in Rocky's skull with horror. He swayed on his feet before tipping over backward. Crashing to the ground, he twitched once or twice before he grew still. Blood spread across the floor in a pool of crimson— the color of death.

Confused, Amelia looked around until she spotted a pale face in the gloom. Light-brown hair curled around a girl's collar, and deep blue eyes stared at Amelia with a mixture of fright and determination. "Amelia? Are you okay?"

"D... Daisy?" Amelia asked, shocked and surprised.

"It's me, but there's no time to talk. We've got to run," Daisy said, prodding Rocky's corpse with her foot. Satisfied that he was dead, she turned to face the open door, standing guard.

Amelia stared at the spectacle, unable to comprehend what her eyes were seeing. "You killed him. You killed Rocky."

"Yes, I shot him. He was going to kill you," Daisy replied, tossing her an impatient look.

CHAPTER 4 - AMELIA

"You… I…" Amelia shook her head. None of it made sense. Sweet young Daisy wielding a gun? Killing Rocky? It wasn't possible. *I must be dreaming. This is a dream.*

"Amelia!" Daisy yelled, her voice sharp. "Get up!"

Daisy's voice cut through the fog in Amelia's brain, and a spurt of adrenalin rushed through her veins. "Sorry!"

"Just hurry. The dead will be everywhere by now," Daisy said.

Amelia jumped to her feet. Blood filled her mouth, the flesh of her cheek cut to ribbons by Rocky's fist. A split lip leaked droplets of crimson down her chin, and she spat out a gobbet of bloody saliva. Her wrists ached, and her ribs twinged from the fall. But there was no time to lick her wounds or feel sorry for herself. Their lives depended on it.

Casting around, she spotted her lost weapon and scooped it up. She gripped the metal pipe with both hands and rushed to Daisy's side. One look into the open was enough to turn her insides to water. "You know we're probably going to die, right?"

"I know, but it's better than doing nothing. If I die, I'm going down swinging," Daisy said with a bloodthirsty grin.

"Alright. I'm with you," Amelia said, setting her chin.

As they headed to the door, a couple of undead faces filled the entrance. Amelia raised her pipe, ready to strike, but Daisy got there first. Bang, bang!

Both infected fell to the floor, their brains turned to mush, and Amelia marveled at Daisy's expert aim. *Who'd have thought? Daisy, of all people wielding a gun like a badass. What's next? Purple zombies?*

"Follow me," Daisy said. Without hesitation, she jumped over the two zombies blocking the doorway and hurled herself into the fray.

Amelia followed, filled with admiration for the girl. While Daisy might be scared, she wasn't letting her fear stop her, and neither would Amelia. *We can do this. We have to.*

Chapter 5 - George

Gripping his ax in his single remaining hand, George nerved himself to dash into the foray, but first, he took care of the man lying at his feet. A quick chop to the temple was enough to ensure the corpse wouldn't reanimate. There was no sense in leaving behind a freshly turned zombie to add to the death and destruction of that night. Dragging the body aside, he took a deep breath, squared his shoulders, and plunged into the night.

A man slammed into his shoulder and sent him spinning, completely off-balance. He fell against the far wall and steadied himself against its smooth surface as more people rushed past. A few were bloody, and he was sure they were infected, but there was no time to worry about that. He had to get to Amelia.

But when a woman carrying a cloth-wrapped bundle ran past, he wavered. A baby's wail reached his ears, and he caught a glimpse of a pink babygrow and tiny fists waving in the air. This triggered his protective instincts, and he glanced at the wall of zombies further down the passage, their progress slow but steady. If not stopped, they'd follow the woman and her baby to the ER and into the night. She wouldn't be safe.

Determined to help, George fell in behind the woman. Every few feet, he'd turn around and make sure the zombies weren't gaining. When a couple of frontrunners got too close for comfort, he turned back and took them out with his ax. It was dangerous but worth the effort—anything to see his charges to safety.

She took a wrong turn at one point, and he yelled, "This way, miss."

"What?" she cried, her eyes wild.

"The exit is this way," he repeated, pointing with his stump.

"Are you sure?" she asked, eyeing the grizzly limb.

"I'm sure," George said, urging her on.

She corrected her course, and he followed her through the ER. The area was deserted, with empty gurneys lining the walls and IV stands casting ghostly shadows on the walls. The smell of antiseptic was strong, but the oncoming infected brought with them a wave of rot and decay, tainting the sterile atmosphere.

Shuddering, George was only too happy to hit the doors, pushing them open for the woman and her baby. They swung shut behind them, and he paused to get his bearings. It was jarring, running out of the relative warmth and shelter of the hospital into the cold, chaotic night. Alarms blared, guards rushed about, Lieutenant Kingsley roared commands over a loudspeaker, and bright spotlights flooded the area, blinding him. The rest of the hospital survivors milled about, uncertain what to do, and he realized it was up to him to see them to safety.

"Over there," George yelled when he spotted the parking lot. It was a hive of activity, and he hoped to commandeer a vehicle for his charges. "Follow me, everyone."

Glad to have someone in charge, the tiny knot of shivering humanity followed him across the open space toward the parking lot. As they drew closer, George was able to pick out individual details.

A group of soldiers under the command of Priya and Blanca were getting ready to evacuate survivors, and a column of vehicles roared to life. Blanca stood on top of a minibus, her rifle held ready across her body, and George guessed she was there to pick off any encroaching infected. More guards surrounded the lot, prepared to fire upon anything undead.

Taking the lead, George ran toward them while waving his arms. Several gun barrels turned in his direction, but the soldiers mercifully had the sense not to fire, and they reached the lot without mishap. Recognizing Priya as the authority, he made straight for her, indicating the small group of survivors with him.

"Priya, these people… can you get them out?" George asked, breathing hard from his exertions.

"Yes, we're evacuating everyone to a secure location," Priya said.

"Thank God," George said, heaving for breath after his exertions.

"Get them onto that bus over there," Priya said, indicating the lead vehicle. "It's fueled and ready to go."

"Okay," George said, turning away. Then a thought hit him, and he whirled around. "There was a bunch of zombies on our tail. They'll hit the exit any moment now, and there's no way to lock the doors," George said, waving toward the ER.

"I'll take care of it," Priya said. Gripping her gun, she waved to a handful of guards nearby. "On me, people. We've got incoming infected."

"Yes, ma'am," came the barked replies, and they stormed off to do their duty.

George hung back, ensuring the woman and her baby got

onto the bus, ready to evacuate. Once everybody was loaded up, he backed away, stopping only when a guard called to him. "Aren't you getting in, Sir?"

George shook his head. "No, I have to go back for my friends."

"Are you sure? This is your chance," the guard said, cocking his head.

"It's okay. Leave my spot for someone else," George said, turning back toward the hospital.

He sprinted toward the ER exit in time to see the zombies hit the set of double doors, pushing them wide open. Priya and her team opened fire as they streamed onto the hospital grounds. A wall of bullets punched into the infected, dropping them like flies. Their bodies shook with the impact, and their skulls exploded like ripe melons.

They fell to the ground one by one until nothing was left standing. The barrage of gunfire slowed then stopped altogether, broken only by the occasional single shot as Priya picked off the last few zombies left writhing on the ground. Too wounded to stand but not quite dead yet.

George stepped forward when the final corpse stilled, its owner no longer filled with unholy life. "Thank you, Priya. The others are on the bus and ready to go."

"What about you?" Priya asked, eyeing his stump and the lone fire ax in his remaining hand. "Why aren't you with them?"

"Because my friends are still inside," George said, waving toward the hospital's interior.

"That's okay; we're going in," Priya said. "We'll get your friends out."

"Sorry, but I'm coming too," George said, setting his jaw.

Priya shrugged. "Your funeral. Just stick close to me, okay?"

CHAPTER 5 - GEORGE

"Okay," George said, tacking himself onto the end of the group.

Priya waved at her team. "Come on, guys. Let's get our people out and make these rotters pay!"

"Yes, ma'am," they roared in answer.

George stuck close to their heels but only planned on going as far as the psych ward. Once he'd rescued Amelia, he'd return for the rest of his friends, but she came first. He'd promised he'd look out for her. A promise made during the long hours they'd spent together in quarantine, and he was not about to break it now.

Chapter 6 - Clare

Clare fell in next to Mason, leading their group to safety. However, they'd only gone a few steps when she had to stop. Her blood-soaked socks kept sliding on the floor, making running nearly impossible.

"Whoa, Bro. Hold up," Clare cried, handing him her ax.

"What now?" he asked, impatience stamped on his features.

"I can't run like this," she said, lifting one foot in the air. With a grimace of disgust, she peeled off the sodden sock and tossed it aside before repeating the maneuver on the other side. "There, that's better."

Mason grunted before he resumed his run to freedom. Setting a brutal pace, Clare worried that some of the others might be unable to keep up. Circling around, she took up a position at the back of the group, ready to help should anyone fall behind.

It was hard to stay focused with the chaotic medley of sirens, screams, yells, and gunshots that filled the hospital. It was even harder to focus on the current goal and not get sidetracked.

Sandi and Paisley might be in mortal danger somewhere in the hospital. The same applied to George, Bobbi, and Amelia, and what about Leo and Sarah, up on the walls outside? But she couldn't worry about them. Not until the rest were safe

CHAPTER 6 - CLARE

and she had a proper weapon.

Suddenly, a different thought occurred to her, and she frowned. How did the dead get out of the morgue in the first place? She'd seen the chains holding the doors in place with her own eyes. There was no way they'd fall off by themselves, and no amount of pushing against them by the undead trapped inside would break them. It just wasn't possible. *What about the stairwells? Maybe they broke through the barricades.*

But that didn't seem likely either. The stairwells had been properly blocked and cordoned off, the opening sealed with sheets of metal and more chains. There was no way the barriers would suddenly weaken and give way unless someone let them out.

Clare's blood ran cold, and she quickly ran to the front of the group again, looking for Mason. She fell in beside him and said, "We have a problem, Bro."

Mason flashed her a quizzical look. "You mean we're not in trouble already?"

"This is not the time for jokes, Mason," Clare answered.

"Sorry," Mason said. "What's the deal?"

"Someone let the zombies out of the morgue or stairwells."

"You think so?" Mason said, slowing down. "They could've gotten loose on their own."

"Not a chance. You've seen those chains and barriers. There's no way this just happened. Someone let the infected out on purpose."

Mason was silent for a few seconds. "You're right. That means we've got an enemy in our midst."

"Or a traitor," Clare replied.

"I've been thinking about it too, and you're right, Clare. This was no accident," Frank said, edging closer to them.

"The question is, what do we do about it?" Mason said.

"We warn Kingsley, and we get our people to the safe house," Clare said.

"What about the rest?" Mason asked.

"We save as many as we can," Clare said. "They're our people too, now."

"Alright," Mason said with a nod. "Let's do this."

They continued down the hallway, only slowing when they spotted a couple of bodies on the floor. Most of the corpses were dead zombies, clearly recognizable by their decayed looks and stench, but a few were fresh—victims of the infected.

"Somebody came through here with an ax," Mason said after briefly examining one body.

"George, maybe?" Clare mused.

"It's possible," Mason replied. "I hope he's okay."

"George is tough. He'll be fine," Clare said. "Besides, he's got Bobbi looking out for him."

"True," Mason said with a grin. "I wouldn't look for trouble with that woman."

"Or her cat," Clare said with a laugh.

"Speaking of, where is that damn cat?" Mason asked. Like Robert before him, he wasn't overly fond of felines.

"Sebastian can take care of himself," Theresa said from the back. "He'll show up out of the blue when this is all over."

"I hope so, for Bobbi's sake," Clare said. Using her ax, she quickly took care of the fresh corpses, ensuring none returned to life.

They continued through the building until they reached the ER but stopped abruptly when a barrage of gunfire sounded straight ahead.

Clare ducked behind the nearest gurney, waving to the rest

of the group to follow. "Get down, get down!"

Bullets whizzed overhead, punching into walls, shattering windows, and clipping furniture. An IV stand toppled over with a crash, and a tray of surgical instruments went flying. Hunkered down, the group took shelter from the fallout, waiting it out.

Finally, the gunfire petered out until it stopped altogether, and a muted hush fell over the area. Voices sounded from outside, and boots crunched on broken glass as somebody picked their way through the trashed entrance.

Daring to take a look, Clare stuck her head out from behind the gurney. "Hello?"

The footsteps stopped, and several gun barrels swung toward her. "Who's there?" a strange voice asked.

"Please, don't shoot. My name is Clare. We're just people trying to get out," Clare replied, swallowing her fright.

"Clare?" another person cried, pushing to the front of the strange group. "It's me, George."

"George? What are you doing here?" Clare asked.

"Long story, but we're here to help."

"Really? Because you were shooting at us just now," Clare said.

"Sorry about that. We were shooting at zombies," a woman replied. "We didn't know you were here. You can come out now, promise."

"Okay, thanks," Clare replied, recognizing Priya, one of Lieutenant Kingsley's SCERT team members.

Relieved, Clare emerged from the gloom, followed by Mason and the rest. "I'm so glad to see you, George."

"You and me both," George replied, shaking hands with Mason.

"Is it safe outside?" Clare asked.

"So far. They've started evacuating people," George said.

"Good. We need to get our people out of here," Clare said.

"What about Amelia? And where's Bobbi?" George asked.

"Bobbi went looking for you. She assumed you'd try to save Amelia," Clare explained.

"I wanted to, but I got sidetracked," George admitted. "I'm on my way there now."

"I'll go with you," Mason said.

"Me too," Clare said.

"No," Mason replied. "You need to get our people out, Sis."

"Why me?"

"Because I trust you," Mason said.

"But I'm not leaving without everyone; Paisley included," Clare protested, anger stirring in her chest. "I'm no coward."

"I know that. Just see our people off to the safe house, take a few volunteers, go to the armory, and grab as many guns as possible," Mason said. "We'll need it to save everyone trapped inside."

"Alright, fine," Clare said, recognizing the sense in his words. "But be careful."

"You too," Mason said.

"Are you lot done chitchatting yet?" Priya asked, shifting from one leg to the other. "We don't have all day."

"Sorry," Mason said. "I'm coming with you."

Priya sighed and removed a sidearm from her belt. "Whatever. Take this."

"Hey, why don't I get a gun?" George protested.

"Because you've only got one hand, and your aim is shit. You're better off with the ax," Priya said. "Now, come on. Let's go."

CHAPTER 6 - CLARE

Without further ado, Priya led the way deeper into the hospital, followed by Mason and George.

Left in charge of the remaining group, Clare looked around. "Alright, folks. We're almost there. Stay close and keep your eyes open."

"Lead the way, Clare," Theresa said. "I know we can count on you."

"Thanks," Clare said, taking the lead.

With careful steps, she picked her way through the field of broken glass and dead zombies until she was in the clear. The others followed, shielding their eyes from the glare of the spotlights.

The grounds were a hive of activity, but the parking lot was the busiest. Rushing over, she found several guards loading survivors onto buses and trucks. Blanca, Kingsley's top marksman, stood on top of a minibus, ready to pick off any infected in the vicinity.

"Where are our vehicles?" Clare asked, looking around.

"Over there," Frank said, pointing to a couple of trucks, cars, and buses in the corner.

"Right, let's go," Clare said, heading toward them.

Along the way, she encountered a harassed-looking Kingsley barking orders through a loudspeaker. He was armed to the teeth, and several guards accompanied him, including Sarah.

"Frank, you're here! You're all here! I'm so glad to see you," Sarah cried, hugging the older man despite his protests. "We were just about to go in and look for you."

"We're okay, Sarah," Frank said gruffly. "But there are still many people trapped inside the hospital."

Rounding on Kingsley, Clare said, "He's right. It's a bloodbath in there. What's the plan?"

"I've already sent in a team through the main entrance—Leo's in charge. Priya's team went in through the ER entrance," Lieutenant Kingsley replied. Waving at Sarah, Chris, and Matt, he added, "We're going in next."

"Just the four of you?" Clare said with a frown.

"We're all I can spare. The rest have to oversee the evacuation and keep the grounds safe. All this noise is bound to draw the city's infected to our doorstep," Kingsley explained.

"We can help," Clare said, indicating herself and a few others. Benjamin, Mike, Elijah, Frank, Timothy, Rick, and Ellen.

"What about me?" Ruby protested.

"Not you. Your medical skills are priceless. The same goes for you two," Clare said, pointing at Theresa and Susan. "You are the best at organizing and caring for large numbers of people."

"You can count on us," Theresa said.

"And I'm grateful for your help," Kingsley said.

"We're in this together, right?" Clare said.

Kingsley nodded. "The armory is open. Arm yourselves and meet us at the entrance of the hospital. We'll be right along."

"You heard the man," Clare said, waving at her group. "Let's move."

Running toward the armory, Clare's blood sang with the familiar thrill of the upcoming battle. While the apocalypse might be hell on earth for most people, it wasn't for her. She relished the sensation of danger and overcoming obstacles. It was what she lived for now, and she couldn't imagine returning to the way things used to be. The only thing she found truly hard was losing someone dear to her, and she prayed that wouldn't be the case today. *Please, God, let Paisley and the others be okay.*

Chapter 7 - Lt. Kingsley

When Clare and her team left for the armory, Lieutenant Kingsley relayed his final orders through his loudspeaker. "Blanca, you're in charge of the guards."

"Yes, Lieutenant," Blanca answered from her perch on top of the minibus.

Satisfied, he turned to Theresa. "You're in charge of the evacuation. Get as many out as you can."

"Of course," Theresa said with a nod.

"There are guards on the walls operating the fifty caliber guns. They are ready to open the gates and take out any infected outside. Coco is preparing the vehicles, ensuring they're fueled and ready to go, and Blanca will keep you safe from any infected while you are loading people onto the vehicles."

"Okay, but where are we taking everyone?" Theresa asked.

It was a pointed question that caused Kingsley to hesitate. "There's a warehouse nearby. Blanca knows where it is. It should suffice for now."

"Suffice?" Theresa said, her eyebrows raising. "Is it safe? Fortified? Supplied?"

"We've reinforced the entrances and placed emergency supplies inside," Kingsley hedged. "Enough to last for a day or two."

"A day or two?" Theresa said, exchanging looks with Ruby and Susan. At a nod from each, she added, "I suppose it will have to do for tonight, but after that, we'd better move everyone to our safe house."

"Your safe house?" Kingsley asked.

"Yes. It's got enough food and water to last a few weeks."

"Weeks?" Kingsley exclaimed.

"We wanted to cover our bases," Theresa said with a shrug.

"Is it safe?"

"As far as it is possible to be in these circumstances."

"And you'd take us there? All of us?" Kingsley asked.

"Of course. We are in this together now. One people, one community," Theresa said.

Her words lifted a weight off Kingsley's shoulders, and he smiled for the first time that night. "Thank you, Theresa. This means a lot to me."

Theresa nodded. "Off you go. There are people inside that hospital that need you now."

"Right," Lieutenant Kingsley said, handing her the loudspeaker.

She gripped the device in both hands. "Godspeed, Lieutenant."

"Stay safe," Kingsley replied, waving to his team. "Come on. Let's go."

He found a jittery-looking Clare dancing from one foot to the other outside the glass doors that lead into the atrium. She was armed with a shotgun, and an additional sidearm rode on her hip next to a fire ax. Her hair was pulled back into a knot, and the pockets of her gray sweatpants bulged with extra ammunition, but her bare feet and baggy clothes struck an odd note.

"No time for shoes, huh?" Kingsley said, raising one eyebrow.

Clare fixed him with a look. "As if the zombies care what I look like."

Kingsley inclined his head. "True, but watch out for ankle biters. They can be really sneaky."

"Thanks. I'll remember that," Clare replied with a grin.

"Ready to go?"

"Oh, we're more than ready," Clare said, jumping up and down.

The rest of the group didn't look quite as eager for battle, but they were locked and loaded. Studying each one, Kingsley was satisfied with their level of expertise and readiness. Clearly, this was not their first rodeo, and they knew how to handle themselves.

"Let's move out," Kingsley said.

He waved his team forward, and they pushed open the doors. The level of noise from inside increased tenfold, assaulting his ears, and the unmistakable stench of rot and decay coated his nostrils.

"Oh, man, that's ripe," Clare said, gagging as she propped open the door with a piece of broken concrete.

"Prepare for the worst," Lieutenant Kingsley said, stepping inside. He pulled his bandanna around his neck up over his nose. The material smelled like stale sweat and bleach, an unpleasant combination, but it blocked out the stench of the undead. "Clear!"

His team moved up with Chris and Matt on either side. Each one carried a flashlight and shone it into the furthest corners, looking for signs of movement. When nothing jumped at them, they continued and entered the main hallway, which led deeper into the hospital.

They advanced through the corridor, checking each room they encountered along the way. Most were empty. Offices and rooms that were long since turned into storage space, but they found a handful of people huddled inside a cleaning closet, squeezed next to shelves.

A woman screamed when they entered, crouching next to two kids. The children burst into tears, and a man jumped up, wielding a broom. "Stay back!"

Two more men and a woman joined him, each holding a makeshift weapon of some sort, and Kingsley found his admiration for the plucky survivors rising by the second. Raising both hands in the air, he shouted, "Whoa there. Calm down. It's Lieutenant Kingsley."

"Lieu… Lieu… Lieutenant Kingsley?" the woman asked, her voice shaky.

"It's me," Kingsley said with a nod. "We're here to help."

The woman's shoulders sagged, and her mop drooped to the floor. "Thank God. We thought you were zombies."

"You can come out now. The way to the exit is clear, and vehicles are waiting to evacuate you," Kingsley said.

"Oh, thank you. Thank you," the woman said with a sob, and Kingsley stepped aside to let her and the others pass.

They filed through the door, a sad little group with frightened eyes and no chance of survival on their own. For the hundredth time that night, Kingsley cursed himself for not ensuring that his people were prepared for the outside world. Untrained and sheltered, they were like lambs to the slaughter.

"Clare, can you and two others please escort them to the exit?" Kingsley asked. "We'll clear up ahead."

"Okay," Clare said, waving to Rick and Ellen. "Let's see these people to safety."

Kingsley motioned the rest of his team onward, and they continued down the hallway, checking rooms and wards as they went. Clare, Rick, and Ellen returned shortly after that, and the search sped up. Twice more, they found groups of survivors hiding in store rooms and offices, and each time, a trio of volunteers escorted them to the exit. It was just a drop in a bucket, however.

Another set of double doors loomed ahead, and Kingsley knew that was where the real trouble waited. Wards B and C lay through there, occupied by his people. That was where he'd find all his friends: Sophia, Lindsey, Stella, Dirk, and many others. A third room hosted the children, parents, and teachers from the fire station. The thrift store and schoolroom were just beyond that, alongside communal bathrooms, a couple of store rooms, the cafeteria, and the kitchen. All of it overrun.

Lieutenant Kingsley could only hope that his people had the common sense to barricade their doors and wait for rescue. Without weapons, they had zero chance of survival in a fight. But what were the odds? When panic struck, the last thing people did was use their heads. It was far more likely they'd done something stupid like try to run.

"All right, guys. Through those doors are our friends, family, community members, and a ton of zombies. Stick together, stay with me, and watch each other's backs. Got it?"

"Got it!"

"Yes, Sir!"

"Yes, Lieutenant!"

Reaching for the door handle, Lieutenant Kingsley prepared himself for the worst. *Here goes.*

Chapter 8 - Theresa

With Lieutenant Kingsley out of the picture, Theresa took swift command of the evacuation. She found a sheltered spot for Sebastian's crate, vowing to get him into the first available bus.

Next, she got the ball rolling. "Ruby. We need to check everyone for infection. The last thing we want is someone turning on a bus full of people."

Raising the loudspeaker to her lips, she cried, "Blanca. You and your guards watch for zombies while we get everyone checked for bites and loaded onto the vehicles."

Blanca nodded and gave a thumbs-up signal from her perch on top of the minibus before turning to the guards scattered around the parking lot. "You heard the lady. Kill anything that isn't human!"

A chorus of scattered replies rang around the space, and Theresa returned to the job at hand. "Susan, line everyone up here and keep them calm. Panic is the enemy of reason."

"Of course," Susan replied with a warm smile. "I'll take care of them."

A woman with spiky black hair and tattoo sleeves covering both arms jogged over, her clothes stained with motor oil. "Are you in charge of the evacuation?"

CHAPTER 8 - THERESA

"For the moment, yes," Theresa affirmed.

"I'm the mechanic and in charge of the vehicles," the woman said.

"Coco?" Theresa asked, recognizing her from earlier board meetings. "That's me," Coco said, flashing a smile laden with silver. She had several studs in her nose, tongue, eyebrows, and ears.

Theresa had often wondered if it hurt, decided it probably did, and that she'd rather not try it for herself. Now, she returned Coco's broad smile and said, "Thank you for your assistance, and keep it coming. We need all hands on deck now."

"Alrighty," Coco said, hurrying away.

"I guess it's just you and me now, Ruby," Theresa said.

Looking around, she spotted a bus already loaded with survivors and ready to go. The vehicle stood at the head of the convoy, the engine idling with a guard behind the wheel. Hurrying over, she knocked on the door and climbed in, followed by Ruby.

"Find a seat and sit down," the driver yelled when he saw them.

"We're here to check for bites," Theresa replied. "Lieutenant Kingsley sent us."

"Alright. Go ahead," the driver replied.

Together, Theresa and Ruby climbed onto the bus and examined each survivor for possible infection. Shell-shocked and exhausted, nobody complained, and everyone submitted to the examination without protest. Finally, they reached the last evacuee, a woman cradling a baby in her arms.

"Are you okay, miss?" Theresa asked.

"I'm okay," the woman replied, her voice hoarse with unshed

tears.

"And your baby?"

"She's scared. She doesn't understand what's going on," the woman said, hiccuping. "I don't understand either. One minute everything was fine. I was up with Emily. She's been fussy all day. Teething. I thought she might settle down if I took her for a walk. Then, they were there in the hallway. The undead."

"I'm sorry," Theresa said. "At least you made it out alive."

"I wouldn't have if it wasn't for the one-armed man. He helped us," the woman replied.

"One-armed man?" Theresa repeated, exchanging a look with Ruby. "George?"

"Could be," Ruby replied with a shrug.

"You know the man?" the woman asked.

"We do. His name is George. Do you know where he is now?" Theresa asked.

"He went back into the hospital looking for someone. A lady named Amelia, I think," the woman replied.

"I see. Thank you very much," Theresa said, squeezing the woman's hand. "The good news is that you are both infection-free and safe. We'll be leaving soon."

"But… where will we go?" the woman asked, her tone growing shrill with panic. "This was our home."

"She's right," a man cried. "Where will we go?"

"The city is overrun. Nowhere is safe," another said.

"Calm down, please. We've got somewhere lined up for tonight. Somewhere safe," Theresa said.

"And tomorrow?" the woman asked.

"Tomorrow, we'll go to a safe house. It's fortified and supplied. There's no need to worry."

CHAPTER 8 - THERESA

"What about the zombies? They're everywhere," the woman protested.

"That's what the armed guards are for," Theresa said. "They'll keep you safe."

"Are you sure?"

"I'm sure," Theresa said with her most reassuring smile.

"Alright. Thanks," the woman said, sinking back into her seat.

As Theresa and Ruby exited the bus, the woman's baby began to cry. Mewling cries that tugged at the heartstrings. In an effort to soothe the child, the mother began to sing—a crooning lullaby, both achingly familiar yet alien in the current setting.

Hush, little baby, don't say a word,
Mama's going to buy you a mockingbird.
If that mockingbird won't sing,
Mama's going to buy you a diamond ring.
If that diamond ring turns brass,
Mama's going to buy you a looking glass.
If that looking glass gets broke,
Mama's going to buy you a billy goat.
If that billy goat won't pull,
Mama's going to buy you a cart and bull.
If that cart and bull turn over,
Mama's going to buy you a dog named Rover.
If that dog named Rover won't bark,
Mama's going to buy you a horse and cart.
If that horse and cart fall down,
You'll still be the sweetest little boy in town.
So hush, little baby, don't you cry,
Daddy loves you, and so do I.

Frozen to the spot, Theresa listened to the haunting melody, her heart breaking in two. It reminded her of everyone they'd lost since the apocalypse began and everyone they still stood to lose. It also reawakened the terrible pain she'd buried since Robert died and Amelia suffered her mental breakdown. It was tragic and unfair, but nothing in life had ever been fair. Not before, and not now.

Unshed tears burned her eyelids, and she dashed them away. There was no time to waste on empty regrets. Not when they had a community to save. "Come on, Ruby. Let's go."

Ruby nodded, her gaze sympathetic. They all felt it. The gravity of the events around them. They would either make it through the night or they wouldn't.

Exiting the bus, they canvassed the rest of the parking lot. There was no news from either Kingsley, Priya, or Leo's teams, and only a trickle of survivors had made it out of the hospital thus far.

One by one, Theresa, Ruby, and Susan checked each one for infection and directed them toward the waiting vehicles. The procedure went smoothly for a while until the inevitable happened.

"Sir, could you stand over there, please? It won't take long," Ruby said, directing a middle-aged man toward the light.

"No. I won't let you touch me," the man said.

"Sir, please. We have to check everyone for infection," Ruby repeated. "It's protocol."

"Protocol, my ass. I know my rights, and I won't let the likes of you touch one hair on my head."

"The likes of me?" Ruby asked, incredulous.

"You're not a real nurse. Just some desk monkey who doesn't know what to look for," the man replied. "I'm not infected."

"If you'll let me examine you—"

CHAPTER 8 - THERESA

"No! Don't touch me!" the man screamed, pulling a knife from his belt. He waved it around, a warning to all not to come close. "Stay back!"

Blanca quickly abandoned her post on top of the minibus and sauntered over, her voice as colorless as her looks. "Drop the knife, or I'll shoot."

"What? You can't!" the man said, growing pale.

"I can, and I will," Blanca said.

"You don't have the authority."

"Try me," Blanca said, looking almost bored.

"Blanca, wait," Theresa said, scrambling for a non-violent way to fix the situation. "He's just scared."

"He's threatening my people," Blanca said, not giving an inch.

Suddenly, an older man wearing khaki fatigues stepped up, his movements a blur. Before anyone could blink, he grabbed the other man's wrist, twisted it hard, and took the knife from his nerveless fingers.

Disarmed, the would-be knife man staggered away, clutching his wrist. "Ow, that hurt!"

"Be thankful I didn't break the bone," the older man said, his tone amused.

"Thank you, Sir," Theresa said, relieved.

"Call me Jakes," the man replied.

"Thank you, Jakes. I appreciate your help."

"Don't mention it," Jakes said, his neat gray beard glinting in the spotlights. "But what do we do about him?"

"I'll take care of him," Theresa said. "Sir, we need to check you now. No more fighting."

"No, I… please," the man said, wringing his hands.

"I've had enough of this," Blanca said, gesturing at two guards hovering nearby. "Check him for bites."

Despite the man's protests, the guards swooped in and gave him a quick once-over. It didn't take long to discover what he was hiding—an ugly bite on his upper shoulder, hidden by his jacket's collar.

Stricken, the man babbled. "Please, don't kill me. I'm not sick."

"Maybe not yet, but it won't be long," Blanca said, raising her gun.

"No, please! I feel fine," the man pleaded, tears streaming down his face.

"I'm sorry, but I have no choice," Blanca said.

"Wait!" Theresa cried. "You can't shoot him."

"Why not?"

"Lieutenant Kingsley wouldn't want that. Not like this."

"So, what do we do with him? What if he turns during the evacuation?" Blanca asked.

"We'll quarantine everyone who's infected," Theresa said. "We can put them on a separate bus with armed guards."

"Until when?" Blanca said.

"Until we can deal with the situation," Theresa said.

"I don't like it. It's a waste of time," Blanca said, clearly not convinced. "Better we end it now."

"Look around, Blanca. Killing this man in cold blood would be bad for morale," Theresa said, waving at the assembled guards and people. "We're not killers."

"I know that, but he's infected," Blanca said. "He's dangerous."

"We'll be careful, I promise, but we have to be humane," Theresa insisted.

Blanca hesitated, her gun wavering. Around her, everyone watched, their expressions wavering between horror, terror, and disinterest.

CHAPTER 8 - THERESA

Theresa knew that killing a man, a living human being, even if infected, would become a tipping point for all of them. It would strip away the last vestiges of civilization and render them utterly lawless. "Please, Blanca. Don't do this."

"Fine," Blanca said, lowering her gun. "Load him up, but zip-tie his hands."

"Thank you," Theresa said, sagging with relief.

"You and you," Blanca said, gesturing to two guards. "Load any infected survivors onto a separate vehicle, make sure they're secured, and watch them. If any of them look like they're about to turn, shoot them."

"Yes, ma'am," the guards replied.

"When the time comes to leave, I'll drive," Blanca said.

Nodding, they hustled the man toward a nearby empty bus, put him in a seat, and tied his hands to the seat with a cable tie.

The moment they were gone, Blanca turned back to Theresa. "I still don't like this idea. You know that man will die anyway."

"Yes, but we're not monsters," Theresa said.

"Maybe not you," Blanca said, her expression unreadable.

Theresa stared at the woman, trying to read her. It was near impossible, and she gave up after a few seconds. Turning her thoughts back to their current predicament, she asked, "Are there any supplies lying around outside?"

"Supplies?" Blanca asked. "Why?"

"We'll need it wherever we go," Theresa said. "People aren't the only thing we should be loading."

Blanca's eyes narrowed, and she was silent for a while. "You are right, of course. I'll see to it."

"Thank you," Theresa said, though she privately thought Kingsley and his team were missing the obvious. While saving human lives came first, keeping them alive was just as important.

"That is one scary woman," a gruff voice said, and Theresa turned around to find Jakes standing behind her.

"That she is," Theresa agreed.

"Need help with anything?" Jakes asked.

"I need all the help I can get," Theresa admitted.

"Tell me what to do, and I'll do it," Jakes said.

Theresa welcomed him into the fold with gratitude and put him to work loading survivors. He proved very good at it, his manner both reassuring and authoritative. People were happy to do as he asked, confident that he knew what he was doing.

Blanca wasted no time either. She quickly rallied the troops, and they loaded whatever was available. There wasn't much: Rolls of barbed wire, metal sheets, fuel drums, some empty and some full, generators, lights, and wiring.

Coco soon realized what was happening and emptied her garage of anything useful. Within minutes, she had a load of spare tires, batteries, power tools, equipment, motor oil, parts, and containers ready to go.

Blanca made a run to the armory, stripping it to the bone. At the same time, another team raided the greenhouse and gardens, removing hoses, pots, water containers, shade netting, gardening tools, and whatever else they could get their hands on.

Finally, it was done, and they settled into a tense state of awareness. On the one hand, the convoy was ready to evacuate. On the other hand, everyone waited for news from inside the hospital and the rest of the survivors. Dozens were still missing, trapped inside the building.

Glancing at her watch, Theresa noted with surprise that only twenty minutes had passed since Kingsley took his team inside.

CHAPTER 8 - THERESA

Twenty minutes that felt like a lifetime. Questions rose in her mind, echoed by Ruby and Susan, who flanked her.

"Do you think they're still alive in there?" Ruby asked.

"Someone is," Theresa replied, wincing when a battery of gunshots tore through the hospital's innards.

"Do you think our people are still alive in there?" Ruby amended.

"They are all our people now, but yes, I'm sure they're alive," Theresa said.

"I'm sure of it, too," Susan said. "They're tough. They'll survive."

"Yes, they will," Theresa replied, keeping her expression calm.

It was necessary to present a solid front to the evacuees. Panic would derail the entire operation and sow panic among the gathered crowd, but deep down, she wondered. *Are they still alive? Why are the radios so quiet? Why haven't more survivors exited the building?*

Chapter 9 - Nikki

With the gas station and its zombies left in the dust, Nikki focused on the road ahead. She'd already mapped out the route the night before, taking care to utilize the back roads. She didn't want to worry about other drivers and hoped that the way she'd chosen would be quiet and free from traffic, especially of the infected kind.

"Only one way to find out, boy," Nikki said, shivering. With winter around the corner, there was a distinct chill in the air, and she quickly cranked up the heat. Once the cab warmed up, she leaned back in her seat. "That's better. Safe and sound."

Cooper agreed, curling up next to her leg. He tucked his nose underneath his tail and soon fell asleep. His soft fur proved tempting, and she ran her fingers through the curly golden strands. Cooper groaned with appreciation, shifting closer.

"Ooh, you like that. Don't you?" Nikki said, grinning.

With the road ahead as clear and straight as an arrow, she stroked his head with her free hand. The activity was soothing, and an air of contentment filled the cab. They were warm, rested, and free from immediate danger; plus, they had a truck full of supplies and a tank full of fuel. Things were looking up.

For the first time in days, Nikki had a chance to reflect on everything that had happened over the past few weeks.

CHAPTER 9 - NIKKI

Looking back, it felt like the blink of an eye. One moment everything was normal, and the next, a whirlwind of death and destruction descended on the country and its hapless citizens. It wasn't an accurate perception, however.

Rumors of an infectious disease circulated for months before the first concrete news reports aired on all the major networks. A rabies-type disease that reportedly drove the host insane, stripping them of their humanity. Governments began to talk about border control and quarantine facilities, scientists started working on a cure, and doomsday preppers headed for the hills. They turned out to be the smart ones in the end.

Even then, nobody that Nikki knew cared. The disease was too far away, infecting strangers in distant countries. The thought of it affecting anyone's life to an actual extent was absurd. Things like that didn't happen in the States, and everyone was sure it would blow over. It was business as usual, and even Nikki dismissed the freaky rumors.

Besides, she had enough on her plate to contend with. Being from the wrong sides of the tracks meant that she was a social outcast, and in her shithole town, that was saying something. With her hand-me-down clothes, alcoholic stepdad, and eat-shit-or-die attitude, nobody cared that she was a straight-A student and a borderline genius in mathematics and science. Nope. She was a nobody, spawned in the gutter and abandoned by her mother. Even her brother ran away, leaving her behind. Nobody cared about her.

That sense of aloneness grew to define Nikki's life, and she soon became a recluse. Avoiding idle chitchat and social media, she was one of the last to hear about the apocalypse. When she did find out, she made the same mistake as all the rest: She ignored it. Rex, school, and studies carried on, but underneath this surface of complacency lay a ticking time bomb. A timer that heralded the end of humanity's reign, ushering in a new era: The rise of the dead.

"We were so stupid," Nikki muttered with a shake of her head. "The warning signs were all there. We just needed to pay attention."

Cooper looked at her with his big brown eyes, and her heart melted. "At least we found each other, boy."

Cooper licked her hand before he laid his head back down and promptly fell asleep again. With the dog as out as a light, Nikki looked at the road ahead. It wound through the trees and grassy hills like a gray snake, its body dipping and rising with the terrain. It began to grow hot inside the cab as the sun rose high in the sky, and she shut off the heat and cracked a window. Fresh air streamed through the gap, and she sucked in a deep breath, feeling better than she'd had in days.

It promised to be a fine day. One of the last of the season, and Nikki was determined to enjoy it to the fullest. Her stomach rumbled, and she was reminded that she hadn't eaten yet. Neither had Cooper. They'd been in too much of a hurry to escape the gas station and its zombies to worry about food.

With that thought in mind, Nikki sought a suitable spot to meet their needs. With hip-high grass on either side, she wasn't comfortable with visibility in the area and kept going, but a couple of miles later, she spied a clearing covered in gravel and pulled over. "I suppose this will have to do. Right, Cooper?"

Cooper sat upright and looked around with a groggy expression. When he saw nothing to alarm his senses, he yawned and sniffed the air.

"Would you like to stretch your legs, boy?" Nikki asked, but it was a rhetorical question. Nature was calling, and her bladder

CHAPTER 9 - NIKKI

couldn't wait much longer. "But first, I have to prepare."

Pulling her gun from its holster, she checked the magazine. Trying to kill the zombie at the gas station had cost her dearly, as had her encounter with Cooper's previous owner. "Damn. Only five bullets left, and with my shitty aim, that isn't much."

The spare gun she'd taken from Cooper's owner only had one shot missing, though, and she decided to take that instead. Tucking it into the holster, she stashed the Glock underneath the seat as a backup. However, that still didn't solve the problem of her lack of marksmanship, and she mulled it over. What to do? What to do?

Finally, she grabbed a hammer, the same one she had taken from her previous home, and hefted it in one hand. Could she do it? Could she take on a zombie in hand-to-hand combat? She'd signed up for Aikido lessons a few months back and religiously attended the classes every week. She hadn't progressed very far, though. Not enough to defend herself against Rex and not enough to take on a full-grown zombie in rage mode.

"But I don't have a choice, do I?" Nikki mused, eyeing the blunt hammer. "I can't keep wasting bullets. Who knows when I might find more?"

Sighing, she climbed out of the truck and surveyed the surroundings. The area was flat, covered in gravel, and the tree line was a fair distance away. "I should be able to see something coming long before it gets to us. Come on out, boy. It's safe, for now."

Cooper barked and jumped out of the vehicle. He hit the dirt in a spray of rocks and circled the clearing with his nose to the ground. Whenever he smelled something interesting, he lifted his leg and peed on it. Soon, puddles of urine marked his new territory, and he returned to her side with a self-satisfied smile.

"Enjoy that, did you?" Nikki asked with a laugh. She lifted a box of food and water from the truck's bed and placed it on the ground. Dropping to her haunches, she rummaged through the contents and removed a can of dog food and a bowl. She opened the can and dumped the contents into the bowl, offering it to the hungry canine. "Bottom's up!"

Cooper jumped at the opportunity and practically inhaled the food, eating so fast she was afraid he would choke. "Slow down, boy. There's no rush." But the dog ignored her, clearly not agreeing with her assessment of their safety. With a shrug, she removed a second bowl from the box and filled it with water. "That should do for now."

With Cooper taken care of, Nikki turned her attention to her empty stomach. A can of peach slices filled the aching void in her belly, and she followed it up with a packet of peanuts and a can of energy drink. Revitalized, she made her way to a small clump of brush and emptied her bladder.

Squatting out in the open with her bare ass in the air wasn't her favorite pastime, and she was glad it was only a pee. Looking back, she thanked her lucky stars for the bathroom at the gas station. "That would not have been cool," she said, wrinkling her nose.

Afterward, Nikki walked around the clearing, stretching her legs. She tossed in a couple of jumping jacks and stretches, aware of the road ahead. She still had a long way to go before she reached Burlington, maybe two or three days travel, and that was without any complications or obstacles along the way.

"Yeah, right. It's the apocalypse. Of course, there will be problems," Nikki said with a snort, and she knew it was true.

CHAPTER 9 - NIKKI

Felt it in her gut. The next few days would test her resolve and reveal whether or not she had what it took to survive. She'd seen enough movies to know it wasn't just the zombies that posed a danger. Other people could be just as vicious, and hunger, thirst, exposure, and disease were ever-present threats. *I have to be careful. Very, very careful.*

Even if she did survive, finding George wouldn't be easy. The last known location she had for him was the firehouse in Burlington, New Jersey. However, the likelihood of him still being there was zero, and she had very little to go on. Still, she was determined to find him, though she was no longer sure about her motivation. She was angry at him for abandoning her when she needed him most. She hated him for leaving her with Rex and despised him for not coming back, but she also loved him and missed him. He was her brother, after all. Her blood. The only thing she had left in the world. *If he's still alive.*

The thought that George might be dead already hit her like a sledgehammer, and she violently shook her head. *No. It can't be. He has to be alive, and I have to find him. We can't leave things like this between us. Broken and ugly. We have to fix it. We have to fix us.*

Determined to find her brother, Nikki whistled to Cooper. "Come on, boy. Time to go."

Cooper squirted one last stream of urine over a patch of defenseless dandelions, obliterating the poor blooms in a wash of pungent yellow liquid. Then he jumped into the cab and claimed his customary seat. Nikki loaded the box of food into the back and climbed behind the wheel.

As the truck slid onto the road, she said, "Don't you dare die on me yet, Brother. We have a lot to talk about; if anyone deserves the right to kill you, it's me. Not the zombies. Me."

Chapter 10 - George

George and Mason followed Priya's team into the hospital, running through the ER. When they reached the far end, they propped open the doors using a couple of empty gurneys. It would facilitate the evacuation of any survivors they came across, a fact proven when they encountered a group of fleeing people.

"Move, move, move!" Priya yelled, waving them past. "The exit is straight ahead."

"Thank you," their leader replied, herding his group through the ER.

"Head to the parking lot," Priya added. "An evacuation is underway."

The man nodded and hurried away.

George watched them go with mixed feelings. Relief that they were on their way to safety and regret that no one he knew was among them. Neither Amelia nor Bobbi.

"Stop daydreaming, George," Mason snapped.

"Sorry," George said, snapping to attention.

He fell in beside Mason, and they moved deeper into the hospital. A knot of zombies rushed them from a side corridor, howling like banshees.

George chopped at the nearest one, and his ax sank deep

into its temple. He wrenched the blade free, and the infected tumbled to the ground. Priya and her team took down the rest with a few well-placed shots, and all resistance disintegrated. Afterward, they picked through the mess of bodies and killed anything that still moved while the rest of the team swept ahead, clearing out any lurkers.

"Stay back," Priya said, warning Mason and George away from the scene. "We'll take care of this."

George frowned, impatience spurring him on. Worry for Amelia lay heavy on his heart, and he wanted to get to her as soon as possible. "We need to move faster."

"We're doing our best," Priya replied with a look of irritation.

"Sorry," George said, trying to look contrite. "Let me help."

"Me too," Mason said.

"No. Just stay back," Priya said, waving them off.

George glared at her but kept his mouth shut. Arguing would not help anyone at this point, but he resented the implication that he wasn't good enough to fight alongside her and her team. *Is it because I only have one arm? Because there's nothing wrong with the one I have left.*

Mason muttered something under his breath, but he also kept quiet. They forged ahead as soon as the way was clear, moving fast. Minutes later, they turned a corner and spotted a three-way junction. Two hallways led to the left and right, with a sign pointing to the psych ward straight ahead.

"Over there!" George cried, rushing forward.

"No, wait," Mason yelled, holding him back.

"What? It's right there," George said, yanking to free his arm.

"Look. What about them?" Mason said, pointing ahead.

George froze when they moved closer, and he saw the crush of bodies that filled the juncture. The crowd surged back and forth, fighting, screaming, howling, and growling. It was nearly impossible to tell what was going in, the scene lit by a single fluorescent bulb shining overhead. The stench made him gag—the sickly sweet stench of death.

Priya rushed into the fray, picking off the closest infected at point-blank range. Her team followed suit, and a barrage of gunfire filled the space. The shots had a galvanizing effect on the crowd. One half turned toward the noise and attacked the team with vicious snarls while the remaining half screamed and stampeded in the opposite direction.

"Stop shooting!" George cried, realizing that the mob consisted of both zombies and survivors. Using guns in such a crowded space was a recipe for disaster, with human casualties as the inevitable result.

"Ah, shit!" Priya yelled, coming to the same conclusion. "No guns! There are civilians in there. Hand weapons only."

She holstered her gun and grabbed her knife, holding it with the blade aligned to her forearm. The guards followed her example, holstering their side arms and slinging their rifles across their backs.

They waded into the mess, hacking, slashing, kicking, booting, and punching. Priya's blade, a monster that would've had Crocodile Dundee green with envy, cut through decayed flesh like a hot knife through butter. She easily cut through their necks, parting ligaments, muscles, and vertebrae. A head flew through the air, scattering drops of blood over the crowd below. It landed with a sodden thud, the mouth still trying to bite at the air.

Mason kicked it aside with a grimace of disgust, and it rolled across the floor like a discarded football. Relying on his ax, he took down two more zombies before he waved to George.

CHAPTER 10 - GEORGE

Whirling around, he waved at George and said, "Come on. The psych ward's on the other side of this mess!"

"Coming," George replied, pushing forward.

An infected grabbed his arm, its decayed fingers wrapping around his wrist. He tried to pull free, but the thing had him in a vice grip. Lifting his foot, he kicked the zombie in the knee. The joint broke, the bones splintered, and the cartilage exploded in a spray of clotted, black blood. A second kick nearly took the leg right off, and the infected fell to the ground with a snarl. The moment it let go of his arm, he took his chance.

Thunk!

The fire ax sank deep into the creature's skull, grating against the bone. Bracing himself with one boot against the creature's chest, George pulled his weapon free. He slammed the blunt end into the face of another, reversed the blow, and hacked through a third zombie's neck.

Suddenly, the crowd rippled. Gunshots rang out, and people screamed. George looked around, confused by the turn of events. Priya and her team were not responsible for the gunshots. Then he spotted two women fighting zombies at the room's far end. One lay into the infected with a steel pipe, her dark hair pulled back into a severe knot, while a blonde shot the fallen with a gun.

Frantic to escape the guns and the zombies, the remaining survivors stampeded toward Priya's team. They surged through the narrow corridor, pushing and shoving in their desperation to reach safety.

"Let them pass," Priya yelled, waving her team aside. "Stop only the infected."

George pressed his body against the wall, making way for

the stampeding mob of people. He watched as they ran toward the exit, glad to see them go. *At least someone will make it out alive tonight.*

When the last one disappeared into the distance, he turned back toward the juncture, relieved to see that most of the infected were dead. A few more milled around, but Priya's team quickly dispatched them, and a broken silence fell across the scene.

"Alright, team. Check for any survivors, and make sure all of the infected are dead. Really dead," Priya said, taking command of the situation.

"Yes, ma'am," they responded.

"The same goes for any victims you find. We do not need a bunch of fresh zombies running around," Priya added. She turned to George and Mason. "Stay back while we clear the area."

"We can help," George said.

"I'd rather not," Priya replied. "Let the experts handle this."

"Experts? You think you're better than us because you've got a badge?" George said. "This is the apocalypse, lady. Your badge doesn't mean shit now."

"I'll thank you to watch your tone," Priya said curtly.

"Why? You're the one who's treating us like a bunch of newbies," George said.

"He's right. We survived for weeks out there, killing zombies and going on raids. We don't need you to tell us what to do," Mason said.

"Fine," Priya said. "Go ahead, but don't blame me if you lose another arm. Or your life."

"Excuse me?" George said, shocked that she'd go there. "You know nothing about me."

CHAPTER 10 - GEORGE

"Come on, George," Mason said, tugging at his arm. "It's not worth it. Let's go."

George resisted the pull but gave in when Mason added, "We're here for Amelia and Bobbi. Remember that."

"You're right, of course," George said, allowing Mason to coax him away from a smug-looking Priya and her team.

They picked their way through the corpses that littered the floor, making their way toward the far side of the juncture. It was a grizzly scene, but neither paid much attention, intent on getting to the psych ward.

Halfway across, George froze when he heard a familiar voice say, "George? Is that you?"

"Amelia?" George asked, looking up.

Two figures emerged from the shadows. The same women he'd seen earlier wielding a steel pipe and a gun. Only now, he was able to recognize the brunette: Amelia.

Chapter 11 - Amelia

The corridor outside the psych ward was in chaos. People stampeded past, blindly seeking refuge from the gnashing teeth and grasping hands that filled the night. They trampled each other in their haste to escape, shoving, kicking, and even punching to get to safety.

Even worse was the number of the undead. The things were everywhere, spreading death like the rotting fungi they were. They overwhelmed their victims through sheer numbers, hidden in the shadows until it was too late.

A couple of flickering lights overhead lit the scene in garish yellow, but it couldn't chase away the darkness.

"Shit! What do we do?" Daisy asked, backing up.

"We fight our way through," Amelia said, raising her pipe.

"I don't think I've got enough bullets," Daisy said.

"Then look for something else to use," Amelia said.

"Like what?"

"I don't know. Anything you can use to bash their heads in," Amelia said. "In the meantime, watch my back."

"Go ahead. I'm right behind you," Daisy said.

They fought their way through the crowd of zombies, one infected at a time. Amelia whacked them with the pipe, disorienting them long enough for Daisy to shoot them in

CHAPTER 11 - AMELIA

the head. However, they weren't making much progress, and Daisy was fast running out of bullets. She stopped taking potshots and instead used the butt of her gun as a club.

Bit by bit, they made their way forward until they reached the three-way juncture. Straight ahead lay the exit, but it might as well have been on another continent. The floor was packed with people, both the living and the dead.

Amelia swept her pipe through the air, tripping an infected. It fell to the floor, and she stabbed it in the head with her pipe. Throwing her entire weight into the blow, she caved in its skull, ending its undead life.

Suddenly, a zombie grabbed Amelia by the arm and yanked her closer, its teeth gnashing at the air. They clipped shut mere millimeters from her face, and terror spurted through her veins.

A stench like rotten eggs washed across her face, and vomit bubbled up her throat. It burned the back of her throat, warm and acrid. She tried to hold it in, but her stomach revolted, and yellow bile splashed across the infected's chest. It snarled, not caring about the gunk running down its shirt. It only cared about the sweet flesh that danced around within its grip, and it leaned in for the kill.

"Get off, you undead fucker," Amelia screamed, punching it in the head with her free hand. Its hold loosened, and she could break free, staggering back on shaky legs.

Daisy stepped in, bashing it on the skull with the back of her gun, and it collapsed to the floor with an unholy groan. "Are you okay?"

"I'm fine," Amelia said, wiping her mouth. She sucked in a deep breath, attempting to steady herself. "There are too many of them."

"I know," Daisy said, her eyes wild. She dragged one hand across her sweaty brow and shook her head. "What now? Back to the psych ward?"

"I don't know," Amelia said, despair weighing her down.

Suddenly, the sounds of fighting echoed from across the hall, and Amelia caught a glimpse of armed figures. Gunfire rang out, causing the crowd to surge in the opposite direction. One looked familiar, but the mob closed in and blocked him from view. Still, she wondered. *George? Was that you?*

Amelia and Daisy were pushed into a corner and assaulted from all sides, but Amelia used her pipe as a barrier. She pushed them away and created a barrier while Daisy lashed out with her hands and feet.

When a frightened young woman ran straight past them, chased by a zombie, Amelia wanted to help. Before she could do anything, the creature caught the woman and tore into the soft meat of her shoulder. Bright red blood spurted from the grizzly wound, and a peal of agony rose from the woman's lips. With the bite came death, and there was nothing anyone could do about it.

"I'm sorry," Amelia whispered, feeling defeated. She watched as the woman stumbled into the distance, still pursued by her attacker. They disappeared around a corner, and she wondered if there was any point in carrying on.

"Don't give up on me now," Daisy said, noticing her sudden change in mood. "Hang in there."

Amelia nodded, reminding herself that she had to be strong. Giving up was not an option. Not ever. "I'm still here."

"Good, because we're getting out of this place. You and me both," Daisy said with a determined look.

As if to prove her point, the crowd thinned. Survivors

stampeded through a gap in the undead's ranks, waved to safety by the armed figures they'd seen earlier.

"What's going on?" Daisy asked.

"Help has arrived," Amelia said, watching as their rescuers destroyed the undead, decimating their ranks.

More survivors took the opportunity to escape and streamed to safety by the dozen, making her heart leap with joy. At least some would make it, if not the young woman from earlier. A few undead stragglers showed up toward the end, determined to spoil the party.

"Let's do this," Amelia said, charging forward.

"Hold on," Daisy yelled, following.

Amelia lashed out with her pipe, stabbing and swiping at anything within reach while Daisy covered her from behind. She used her gun when she could and her feet and fists when she couldn't.

One snarling face after another lurched into view. Cold, clammy fingers grasped for their skin, and rotten teeth snapped open and shut like so many piranhas. Finally, the last of the undead fell, and they were left heaving for breath and covered in sticky sweat.

"Is it over?" Daisy asked, sucking in a lungful of air. She choked and doubled over, coughing and hacking.

Amelia slapped her on the back. "Are you alright? Don't die on me now."

"Ugh. I'm fine," Daisy said once she caught her breath. She straightened up, and they turned toward their saviors.

A few were checking the bodies, dispatching any zombies that still showed signs of life, and delivering a mercy stab to those who had fallen victim to their attacks. There were no wounded. The infected had done their job too well.

Two of the group were picking their way through the debris, straight toward Amelia and Daisy.

Honing in on them, Amelia recognized the nearest figure and burst out, "George? Is that you?"

"Amelia?" the man replied, and she instantly recognized his voice. That and the stump where his right hand used to be.

George rushed toward her, his expression one of relief. He reached out with his one good hand, realized it still held a bloody ax, and settled for an awkward thump on the shoulder with his bandaged stump. "Thank God you're still alive. I came as fast as I could."

"Oh? You're the one who left me here to rot," Amelia said, anger stirring within her chest.

George frowned. "I never abandoned you. I was let out of quarantine. "

Amelia frowned. "You never said goodbye."

"I didn't get the chance, but I never left you. I've been trying to get you out of your cell, and when all this shit went down, I came straight here," George explained.

"You did?" Amelia asked, not sure whether she could believe him or not. She still felt resentment at being left behind, rational or not.

"I'd never abandon you," George replied, stepping closer. "We're friends. That's why I'm here. To save you."

"He's telling the truth," the second figure said. One she recognized as Mason.

"Mason? You're here too?" she asked, surprised to find herself close to tears.

"Of course we are. We're family," Mason said, drawing her into a hug.

"Well, you got here just in time," Amelia said.

CHAPTER 11 - AMELIA

"Where's Rocky? He said he'd get you and Beatrice out of here," Mason asked.

"I don't know where Beatrice is, but Rocky is dead," Amelia said, her voice flat. "He almost ate my face off. Daisy saved me. I'd be zombie chow if it weren't for her."

"That's me. Daisy, at your service," Daisy said, stepping forward.

"We owe you one, Daisy," Mason said.

"Have you seen Bobbi?" George asked. "She came looking for me, knowing I was headed here."

"No, sorry. I haven't seen her," Amelia said.

"Sorry to break up this little tea party, but we have work to do. Are you in, or are you out?" a new voice said.

George frowned. "This is Priya. She's Lieutenant Kingsley's second-in-command."

"I know who she is," Amelia said. "I'm crazy. Not stupid. Plus, I had visitors who told me about this place." Fixing Priya with a baleful glare, she added, "And what do you mean, in or out?"

"This is a rescue mission. There are people trapped inside the hospital. Are you coming or not?" Priya asked.

Amelia exchanged a look with Daisy. "If there are people trapped inside, I'm in."

"So am I," Daisy said.

"Well, I didn't save your ass just to let you die now," George said.

"What are we waiting for?" Mason agreed.

"Great. Let's get a move on," Priya said, turning away. She waved to the rest of her team, and they fell in around her like a well-oiled machine.

Amelia took a firm grip on her pipe and followed their lead.

As they ran toward what could very well be certain death, she was shocked to find herself feeling both exhilarated and alive.

Not only was she out of the psych ward, but she was reunited with her friends. Weighed against that, a building full of zombies didn't seem so bad.

Chapter 12 - Bobbi

Bobbi ran through the hallway, her gun clutched in both hands. She was wide awake and alert, ready to take on anything. Avoiding the main hallways, she took a circuitous route to the psyche ward, certain that George would be there. She hadn't missed his devotion to Amelia, a friendship built during many long hours spent together in the loony bin.

Not that either of them belonged in that place. That was a piece of bureaucracy that should've died with the government. It was one more reason to dislike the hospital and its leadership. They clung to the old ways, not realizing they were gone.

Locking their dead up in the morgue was another stupid move, and she wasn't surprised the things- got loose, although she wondered who pulled the plug. Someone had done it, that was for sure, and that someone wanted all of them dead.

As she ran, Bobbi wondered why she cared so much about George. He was more trouble than he was worth. A little shit most of the time and annoying as hell. Especially when he almost got himself killed.

It was a question she didn't have the answer to. Maybe she felt responsible for him after saving his ass on the freeway on day one of the apocalypse. Or perhaps he reminded her of her son. The boy she'd loved and lost when he was barely eighteen.

Either way, she knew she had to find him and make sure he was okay.

Earlier that night, Bobbi had been unable to sleep. Something felt off, and she kept rolling around in her bed. Finally, she gave up and got up, opting for a quick shower while everyone else slept.

Back in the ward, she noticed George's absence. This was not unusual as he often had trouble sleeping too. Still, something was off, and she decided to trust her gut. It had never let her down before.

Moving fast, she pulled on clean clothes and her boots and tied up her hair. Next, she located Sebastian, put him in his crate, and checked the load on her gun.

When the alarm sounded, she was ready. While the rest got themselves sorted out, she locked and barricaded the doors. By the time the horde hit their area, they were prepared and ready to fight their way out.

Handing Sebastian off to Theresa was hard. Maybe the hardest thing she'd had to do in a while, but she trusted Theresa. *She'll look after him. I know she will.*

With her feline friend in good hands, Bobbi focused on her next goal: Finding George. *You'd better still be alive, George or I'm killing you with my bare hands.*

Despite her bravado, the tension was wearing on her. The shadows appeared to pulse with menace, and she imagined zombies jumping out at her. Peering around each corner, she checked that the hallway was clear before she dashed to the other end. It was exhausting, and she began to doubt herself. *Maybe, I should've stayed with the others. George is a big boy. He can take care of himself.*

But Bobbi wasn't the kind to give up. She had to keep going,

CHAPTER 12 - BOBBI

keep trying, and she edged along the wall one step at a time. The sounds of fighting, screaming, and shooting were getting closer, and she paused to get her bearings. While she knew she was moving in the right direction, she might have taken a wrong turn. "Shit, shit, shit. What do I do?"

Suddenly, the stench of decay filled her nostrils, and she whirled around. The corridor behind her was blocked by a mob of undead slowly advancing toward her. They snarled when they spotted her, their ruined faces hideous to behold. Despite their broken bodies, they quickly closed the distance, and she found herself on the run.

Turning a corner, Bobbi almost fell when she found herself facing another wall of infected. Backtracking, she dashed down a different corridor, only to find herself lost within the hospital's labyrinthine innards.

"Shit, where am I?" she cried, looking for a way out. The infected continued their remorseless advance on her location, drawing ever closer. The only way out was straight ahead, or so she hoped until running footsteps alerted her to the presence of another. A man ran toward her, his expression wild. "They're coming!"

"What?" Bobbi said, reaching out to stop and question him, but he shrugged her off.

"Run!" he yelled. "They're coming!"

"Not that way! There are—" Bobbi said, trying to warn him.

He ignored her and disappeared around the corner, straight into the arms of the oncoming dead. Seconds later, she heard him scream, caught in their trap. His agonized screams cut through the air and sawed into her brain, sending a spurt of terror through her veins until they stopped abruptly.

Bobbi looked around, realizing she was trapped. There were

zombies in every direction, and she had nowhere to hide, but she couldn't give up. She didn't have it in her to lay down and die. "There has to be something. Think, Bobbi. Think!"

Staring down one hallway, she suddenly noticed a door. It was only a few feet away from the advancing wall of zombies, and she'd have to run fast if she hoped to make it. "Here goes nothing!"

With her gun aimed at the infected, Bobbi sprinted down the corridor. The distance between them shrank, and her heart bounced inside her chest like a frightened jackrabbit. *Faster! Faster!*

One zombie outpaced the rest, and it reached the door a millisecond before she did. Not stopping, Bobbi shot it at point-blank range, ignoring the splatter of gore that hit her in the face. She grabbed the handle, pushed it open, and fell into the space beyond. Tripping over a stack of buckets, she found herself trapped inside a supply closet with no way out. "Oh, shit!"

She whipped around to push the door shut again, but a dozen bodies thudded into the barrier. Arms thrust through the gap, followed by decayed faces filled with rotting teeth. "No, no, no, no, no!"

Bobbi pushed as hard as possible, her feet sliding on the smooth tiles in a vain search for purchase. She slipped, the gap widened, and more arms burst inside. Cold, dead fingers grabbed hold of her arm, and she shrieked as they dragged her closer to the opening.

Resisting with all her might, she tried to pull free, but the zombies were strong. Too strong. Their diseased faces loomed large, and they groaned with longing for her delectable flesh. Desperate to escape, she tried to shoot, but the angle was too awkward. "Help! Somebody help!"

Sharp teeth sank into her forearm, ripping out a chunk of meat big enough to expose the bone. A second mouth closed on her wrist and tore through the muscles and ligaments while a third crunched down on her fingers.

Bobbi screamed as red-hot pain exploded through her nerve endings, and the gun clattered to the floor. Hot blood poured from the wounds, rendering her arm slippery, and she was able to yank it free. Cradling the mangled limb to her chest, she sank to the floor, sobbing for help. "Help. Somebody help, please!"

Spurred on by her cries, the zombies pushed harder against the door. It slid open another inch, and she kicked out with both legs. One found a foothold against a shelf, and the other slammed into a pile of buckets. With her back pressed to the door, she kept her legs straight and the infected out, but she could only hold it for so long. "Somebody... help! Please!"

But nobody came.

The minutes ticked by, and her body weakened. Her legs began to shake, the muscles burning with the effort. Blood loss made her head spin, and the sheer agony almost caused her to pass out. Losing hope, she called out one last time. "Please, is somebody out there?"

No one answered, and Bobbi sagged with despair. Her life flashed before her eyes, a series of events both happy and sad. There was her wedding, a sunny day full of promise. There was the birth of her son, the only creature she'd ever loved unreservedly. Then there was the accident where a drunk driver stole the light from her life. Grief and anger prevailed, leading to a divorce and bitter recriminations. All she left was her garden and her animals. Now, she had nothing. *I'm going to die here. Torn to shreds like a slab of meat.*

Bang!

Bang, bang!

Zombies snarled, bodies thudded to the floor, and the weight against the door lifted. Silence settled over the space, broken only by the sound of footsteps and hushed voices.

"Hello? Is anybody in there?" someone asked.

"I… I'm here," Bobbi answered, her voice hoarse with pain.

Bitter tears stung her eyelids. Saved or not, her life was over. The virus was spreading through her veins, injected into her bloodstream by a trio of bites. She sagged to the side, and the door opened. Hands dragged her out of the cleaning closet and into the light, examining her wounds.

"Oh, my… Bobbi! Wake up!" a familiar voice dragged her from unconsciousness.

"George?" Bobbi asked, blinking. "Is it you?"

"It's me," he said, his expression pale. "Hold on. We'll get you some help."

"No, don't bother," Bobbi said, shaking her head. "It's too late."

"No, it's not," George said. "We just need to get you outside."

"It's too late," Bobbi said. "I can feel it inside my veins, wriggling around like a worm. A diseased worm."

"We can cut off your arm. I can make a tourniquet. Priya, your knife," George called out.

"George, no. You'll only prolong her suffering," Priya said, her voice soft and sympathetic.

"Damn you!" George swore, turning back to Bobbi. "Tell her you're alright. Tell her you can handle it. You're strong."

"Strong? Not so strong anymore," Bobbi said with a chuckle, but it became a hacking cough. The pain increased tenfold, and she wanted the suffering to stop. "Kill me, please."

"No! Don't give up on me, Bobbi," George insisted. "Listen to me, please. We can still save you."

"It's too late. Let me go, George." The words were slurred, and Bobbi's head lolled against her chest. When she spotted Amelia, she smiled. "You found her. I'm glad."

"Mason! Help me get her outside," George said, refusing to give up. "Ruby—"

"Ruby can't save her," Mason replied, cutting George short. "Look at her. It's too late."

"He's right, George," Amelia said. "Listen to her. She's talking to you."

"George, please," Bobbi said, waving him closer.

"I… I can't lose you, Bobbi. You're my friend. You saved my life," George said, tears streaming down his face. He gripped her uninjured hand with his, holding tight.

"I've had a good run, George, and it's time to let me go. Who knows? I might even get to see my son again."

"Your son? You had a son?"

Bobbi nodded slowly and painfully. "He died years ago, and I still miss him. Every day."

George stared at their intertwined hands, his expression stricken. "I'm sorry. I never knew."

"I never told you," Bobbi said. "But you remind me of him."

"Yeah? How so?"

"You're both annoying. Always getting into trouble," Bobbi said with a faint smile.

George laughed, though it was harsh. "That's me, alright."

Bobbi sobered and fixed him with a stern look. "You have to end it. It hurts, and my death will be long and slow. I don't want that, and I don't want to turn into one of those things either."

"I… I don't think I can," George said, shaking his head.

"Then help me do it," Bobbi said.

George swallowed hard before he nodded. He let go of her hand and took the gun proffered by Mason. Placing it in her palm, he folded her fingers shut with one on the trigger.

Bobbi stared at the weapon. The metal felt cold and smooth to the touch. Heavy, but familiar. With George's help, she raised it to her temple. His trigger finger closed over hers, ready to lend his strength.

"Say when," George said, his voice heavy with sorrow.

"I'm sorry, George," Bobbi said, blinking away sudden tears.

"It's okay," he replied.

Closing her eyes, she sucked in a deep breath and said, "Now."

Her finger tightened on the trigger, and everything went black.

Chapter 13 - George

The gun bucked in his hand, the shot like a flash grenade in his brain. His ears sang, and the weapon clattered to the floor. Bobbi sagged to the side, half of her head blown away. Her expression was vacant, devoid of the person she used to be, vital and alive. A woman who took no nonsense from anyone but also had a heart of gold hidden underneath her tough exterior.

"Bobbi? Bobbi, no," George whispered, horror coursing through his veins. He couldn't believe what had happened or what he'd done. "I killed her. I killed my friend."

"She was already dead," Amelia said. "You simply ended her pain."

George shook his head. "She was my friend."

"I'm sorry, but he can't go on. Not like this," Priya said, her tone surprisingly gentle. "Take him back. Make sure he gets on a bus. He's done enough for the night."

"What about you?" Mason asked.

"My team and I will carry on. There are still many trapped inside," Priya said.

"Good luck," Mason replied.

"Same to you," Priya said before she waved her team onward. They ran into the gloom and disappeared around a corner.

Shocked and dazed, George allowed Mason to pry him away from Bobbi's corpse. His arms were covered with her blood, the crimson fluid slick and warm against his skin. His gaze fell on the awful rents in her flesh, and he shuddered. *She must've been in so much pain.*

Maybe what he'd done had been merciful.

Stumbling through the corridors in a haze, George barely registered his surroundings. Other people overtook them, running for the exits, but he didn't care.

"Come on, George. We're nearly there," Amelia coaxed.

"Steady on your feet, buddy. Just a few more steps," Mason added, leading him onward.

Daisy gravitated around them like a satellite, her gun held ready to shoot anything that threatened them.

Finally, they crossed the ER and burst into the night. The air was brisk, and a cold wind swirled through the parking lot. The garish spotlights were bright. Too bright after the gloom of the hospital. Almost blinded, George had to trust his companions to lead him to safety.

As they neared the evacuation point, several figures rushed over. In the lead was Theresa, followed by Ruby and Susan. The trio surrounded them with cries of relief and joy, but that quickly turned to horror when they noticed a blood-soaked George.

"George? Are you hurt?" Theresa cried.

"It's not mine," he mumbled in reply.

"Not yours? Then…."

"It's Bobbi's. She's gone," Amelia replied.

"Not Bobbi. She can't be dead," Theresa exclaimed, her expression stricken.

"I killed her. I shot her," George said, guilt filling his chest.

CHAPTER 13 - GEORGE

"What?" Theresa cried.

"It was a mercy killing," Amelia explained.

"Oh, I'm so sorry. You poor dear," Theresa said, pulling George into a bear hug.

George allowed her to hold him, and her warmth soaked into his soul. She smelled like lilacs and soap, a scent that reminded him a little of his mother. For a moment, he felt less broken.

"I think he's done for the night," Mason said.

Silently, George agreed with his assessment. *I am done. Just done.*

"Let me examine him, and we can get him on a bus," Theresa said, checking him for infection. After a few seconds, she gave him a thumbs-up. "You're clean. Let's get you loaded up."

She hustled him toward a waiting vehicle and directed him into the nearest seat. "Wait right here, George."

George snorted. Where could he go? He didn't even have the strength to move. Should a zombie attack him at that second, he wouldn't be able to lift a finger to defend himself.

Staring into the night, he waited, his hand lying in his lap. Bobbi's blood dried on his skin, pulling the hairs and causing it to itch. He rubbed his arm against the seat in front of him, almost without noticing.

Outside, the world kept moving, but he felt removed from it. None of it made any sense to him. The people were like ants, running around without rhyme or reason. It could almost be funny if it weren't so tragic.

The door to the bus opened, and Theresa climbed on, followed by Amelia. Theresa carried something in her hands, a box-like shape, and he frowned. "Is that... Sebastian?"

"Yes, this is him. Bobbi gave him to me before...." Theresa hesitated.

"Before she died," George said bluntly.

"Will you look after him for me? For Bobbi?" Theresa asked, handing him the carrier.

George stared through the bars, straight into the green eyes of Sebastian. The poor animal looked scared to death, and a sudden lump formed in George's throat. "It's okay. I'll take care of you now."

Sebastian meowed in reply, and George crumbled. Tears coursed down his face, and he broke into sobs. "I'm sorry, Bobbi. I'm so sorry."

Amelia sat down next to him. "It's okay, George. Let it out. Let it all out."

With her arms wrapped around him and Sebastian on his lap, George cried for his loss. He cried for his friend and a life cut too short, too soon. *May you rest in peace, Bobbi.*

Chapter 14 - Sandi

Sandi woke to the sound of screams ringing in her ears. She jolted awake and shot upright, the blankets clutched to her chest. Blinking her eyes, she looked for the source of the terrified screams, but it was hard to see anything in the dark. However, it was not difficult to understand that something was wrong, and she immediately sprang into action.

Throwing the sheets aside, she scrambled out of bed and shoved her feet into her tennis shoes. Thankfully, she slept fully dressed and wore jeans, a t-shirt, socks, underwear, and a jersey. Next, she tied her hair into a ponytail, grabbed the gun she kept under her pillow, and belted it on.

All around Sandi, the ward was in disarray, woken the same way she had been, terrified and confused. Unlike her, they milled about in confusion or remained frozen in their beds. The screams didn't stop; they intensified in pitch until she thought her eardrums would pop.

"Sandi? What's happening?" Claudia called from the bed next to her.

"I don't know, Claudia, but I think we're under attack," Sandi replied, scratching in her bag for a flashlight.

"Under attack?" Claudia replied. "That's impossible!"

"Nothing is impossible," Sandi said, her fingers closing on

the flashlight, much to her relief. She switched on the light and shone it at the entrance.

A dozen figures thronged the space, pushing and shoving each other in their eagerness to get inside. They swarmed the beds closest to the door. Their victims struggled, trapped by a dozen sets of hands and teeth, and their horrified screams turned into agonized wails.

Sandi paled at the sight, and her knees turned to water. "Oh, shit!"

"What?" Claudia cried. "What's going on?"

"Zombies. They're here," Sandi said, slinging her bag onto her back. Inside, she kept a few things in case of emergency. Extra socks, underwear, a jacket, a knife, a bottle of water, a hairbrush, a toothbrush, batteries, and bandages.

"They can't be. We're supposed to be safe here," Claudia said, shaking her head.

"Uh-huh. Get up, Claudia. Hurry!"

"No! This is crazy," Claudia protested. "Where are the guards?"

"There aren't any guards," Sandi said. "Now, come on. Move!"

"I'm not going anywhere," Claudia said, huddling deeper into the blankets. "I'm staying here until someone comes."

Growing impatient, Sandi rounded on the woman. "When will you get it? Nobody's coming. Nowhere is safe. Ever. That's why I sleep with my clothes on. That's why I have a bug-out bag. That's why I took gun lessons from Frank while you did nothing, relying on others."

Claudia gaped at her, clearly taken aback.

"Now get your ass out of bed, grab a weapon, and follow me. We have to get to the kids," Sandi said.

CHAPTER 14 - SANDI

"The kids?" Claudia echoed, still not moving.

"Ugh, whatever," Sandi said, whirling toward the exit. Whether or not Claudia helped, she had to get to the children. They slept in a smaller room next to her ward and were in danger. That was all that mattered, and she couldn't afford to waste time babysitting scared adults.

Pulling her gun from its holster, she sprinted toward the exit. Along the way, she tried to rouse the others and get them moving. It was their only shot at survival. "Wake up, people. We've got zombies inside! Zombies!"

A few of them were awake, realizing the danger and reacting accordingly. They fell in around her, armed with an assortment of weapons: Guns, knives, baseball bats, and more. James popped up at her side, and she was never happier to see another person in her life. "Thank God you're here, James."

"I've got your back," James said, "but how did these things get inside?"

"I don't know, but we'd better get to the children," Sandi said.

"We'll have to fight our way to them," James said, looking determined.

"I know, but we're all they've got," Sandi said, gripping her gun a little tighter.

They ran toward the crowd of infected, Sandi's flashlight bouncing up and down like a rubber ball. When they got close, she paused, aimed, and fired.

An infected fell, its skull blown to bits, and she felt a moment of gratification. All the afternoons spent under Frank's tutelage were paying off. She shot another and another, but for each one that dropped, more zombies took its place. There was no time to stop and gloat, only fight.

Close to the entrance, Sandi's spotted a woman sprawled in

her bed, eyes wide and unseeing. Her sheet was stained with blood, her stomach a gaping wound with the ribs exposed to the light. More blood dripped and pooled on the floor, a river of crimson.

Sandi sidestepped the pool of blood and hit a zombie on the head with the butt of her gun. It snarled and kept coming, a gash across its forehead weeping black fluid. She kicked it in the stomach and put distance between it and her—enough for James to step in and blow its head to smithereens.

Grabbing her arm, he pulled her toward the exit. "Come on. We need to hurry."

"Right behind you," Sandi replied.

She followed him into the hallway, shadowed by a handful of others. The rest stayed behind, overwhelmed by terror. Unwilling to fight, they were trapped inside the ward. Like rats in a cage, they died at the hands of the infected, their screams spurring Sandi and her group to greater speed.

Outside the ward, the hospital was in shambles. An alarm blared, people ran around like headless chickens, trying to avoid the lurching figures of the undead while others tried to fight back. Sadly, they were inexperienced fighters, untrained and sheltered. Faced with the horror of the undead, most of them crumbled.

Sandi and her group headed straight to the kids' room and burst inside, fearing the worst. She hit the light, and the bulbs overhead flickered to life. With her gun held ready, she waited.

"Over there," James cried, pointing across the room.

Sandi followed his direction and almost cried with relief when she spotted Paisley, and the rest of the kids huddled in the far corner. "Paisley!"

She rushed forward, holstering the gun. She grabbed Paisley

by the shoulders and studied her face. "Are you okay? Are you hurt?"

"I'm okay," Paisley said, her lips quivering. "Are there monsters inside?"

"Yes, sweetie, but we won't let them hurt you," Sandi said.

She turned to James and lowered her voice. "What now? Where do we go?

"We get the hell out of here," James said. "The longer we stay, the bigger our chances of being overrun."

"Okay, I'll take two. One in each hand," Sandi said.

They quickly divided up the children between her and the other teachers. It would be their job to herd the kids out. James and the others would form a protective wall around them, keeping them safe from the undead. That was the theory, and Sandi prayed it would work. If not, she'd start shooting and blast her way out of the building. One way or another, she was determined to get her charges to safety.

Once they were ready to move, Sandi said, "Go ahead, James. We'll be right behind you."

James nodded and ran for the exit. Sandi followed with a kid in each hand, moving as fast as possible. Sticking together, the group left the room and headed toward the hospital's main entrance. To get there, they had to cross a large open space, traverse several corridors, and exit into the parking lot—a near-impossible task.

"Come on, kids. Keep going. Don't stop, okay?" Sandi said, urging her charges onward.

The going was tough because half of the crowd had the same idea while the rest stampeded deeper into the hospital. Caught between two opposing forces, they struggled to make any progress, but they also refused to give up. They couldn't quit. If they did, they'd all die.

"This way, guys," James said, swerving to the side.

Sandi pulled Paisley and the other boy by the hand, making them run even when they wanted to stop. Both bawled like babies the entire way, but she ignored them.

They were about halfway across the space when another group burst through the set of double doors. They were armed to the teeth, hacking and slashing at everything within their reach.

Sandi immediately recognized the leader, and her hopes soared through the roof. "Leo! Over here!"

Leo heard her calls, and his head swiveled toward them. He waved his team in their direction, and they cut their way through the multitude of the undead until they surrounded Sandi's group.

"Are you guys okay?" Leo asked, studying each of them in turn, no doubt looking for signs of infection.

"Much better now that you're here," Sandi replied with a grin.

"This isn't over yet. We still have to get you lot out of here," Leo said, his expression grim.

"Can you?" Sandi asked, ever hopeful.

"Yes, but where are the rest of you?" Leo asked.

"This is it from our ward," Sandi said. "I don't know about the hospital people."

Leo nodded, his eyes roving the scene. He pointed to a sheltered corner and pulled them into it. After forming a rough barricade around them using loose furniture, he assigned his team to their protection. Taking only three people with him, he said, "You wait here while I look for more survivors. As soon as I'm back, we'll get everyone out."

CHAPTER 14 - SANDI

"Promise?"

"Promise," Leo said,

"Please, hurry," Sandi said, her heart beating a mile a minute.

He ran off, disappearing into the crowd. Sandi watched him go with mixed feelings. On the one hand, she understood his need to look for more survivors, but she also wished he'd considered them first. *Please, hurry.*

Thankfully, Leo returned not long after with more people in tow. They looked like Sandi felt: Shell-shocked and terrified. She recognized Hospital Board members Lindsey, Madeleine, and Dirk among them, but the rest were strangers.

"Can we leave now?" she yelled at Leo.

"I'm afraid not," Leo said, shaking his head.

"Why not?" Sandi asked.

"Look around you. We're trapped," Leo said, pointing around the room.

Sandi watched, and her heart dropped to the floor. Leo was right. The undead's numbers had doubled in the short time he was gone. The space between them and the doors had filled with the creatures, cutting off their escape. They weren't going anywhere.

Chapter 15 - Lt. Kingsley

Lieutenant Kingsley shoved open the doors and threw himself through the opening. The space was filled with infected, their snarling faces a hideous sight. They shifted and surged like a tidal wave, shoving and trampling each other in their eagerness to get to fresh meat. Corpses littered the floor, and it wasn't easy to keep one's footing.

Kingsley immediately spotted a group of zombies feeding on a woman, her eyes wide and vacant, blood bubbling from her lips. He ran closer and shot the infected with his rifle, a barrage of bullets that cut through their ranks like a hot knife through butter.

Hands clutched at his collar, and he whirled around, using the butt of his rifle as a weapon. He busted the infected's nose and pulverized its lips. A couple of teeth went flying, and he shoved the creature away. A quick bullet to the brain ended its undead life, and he moved on to the next.

Another grabbed his wrist. Its jaws snapped shut on his sleeve, and pain radiated up his arm. He clubbed it in the head, and the zombie fell back with a snarl.

Whirling around, Kingsley smashed his way through the infected ranks, looking for survivors. A scattering of gunshots, yells, and screams from across the room drew his attention,

CHAPTER 15 - LT. KINGSLEY

and he waved at Clare and the rest of his team. "Over there!"

They yelled in response and surged across the floor, fighting to reach the survivors. Within minutes, they made it to a corner of the room barricaded off with overturned desks, chairs, gurneys, wheelchairs, and other debris. Behind the barrier huddled a group of frightened people, protected by a handful of armed guards.

A bloodied Leo led them, his skin tinged gray with exhaustion. When he spotted Kingsley, his expression brightened, and he cried, "Lieutenant! You're just in time."

"Hold on!" Kingsley replied. "We'll come to you."

"Don't worry, we're not going anywhere," Leo said, fending off three infected with his rifle.

Kingsley pushed forward, aided by his team. Together, they cut through the mob, killing one zombie after another. They used their fists, boots, rifle butts, and melee weapons, unable to fire their guns so close to other survivors. Slashing, hacking, punching, and kicking, they moved across the floor in a single unit.

To Kingsley's surprise, Clare and her team fell in seamlessly. Despite having no formal training, they fought like lions, side by side with the rest. At one point, he spotted Clare howling like a banshee each time she cut down a zombie. Her fighting spirit was admirable, and Kingsley wished he'd met her when he was ten years younger and the world wasn't ending.

Throwing his head back, he mimicked Clare and howled with battle fury. A spurt of adrenalin granted him extra strength, and he waded through the undead crowd like a battering ram.

The infected fell by the dozen. By the time he reached Leo's group, his clothes were soaked in blood and guts. The stench was horrific, even through the bandanna tied around his face. Clapping Leo on the shoulder, he asked, "Are you okay?"

"We're fine, but we're out of ammunition," Leo replied.

Kingsley handed him an extra clip. "That should do you."

"Thanks," Leo said, reloading.

Kingsley surveyed the survivors behind Leo, recognizing a few familiar faces. Madeleine Koch, the matron. Lindsey, their resident cook. Dirk, the engineer. There were more people that he didn't know and a handful of kids. They all looked shocked and frightened. Defenseless.

"Is this all there is?" he asked.

"The only ones still living," Leo replied grimly.

"No one else?" Kingsley asked, aghast.

Leo shook his head. "Even if there are more survivors, we'd never get to them in time. We're seconds away from being completely overrun."

"Alright. Let's get these people out of here," Kingsley said. "Clare, Leo, you two take the lead. The rest of you, form a wall around the survivors and keep them safe."

"Yes, Sir!" came the scattered replies.

"Whatever you say, Lieutenant," Clare yelled with a cheeky grin.

"What about you, Lieutenant?" Leo asked, frowning.

"I'll be right behind you, watching your six," Kingsley replied.

Leo hesitated, but time was running out. The number of infected was growing, with fresh new zombies adding to the ranks of the undead. Soon, it would be impossible to get out.

Spurred onward by Kingsley, Leo moved to the front of the group. He joined up with Clare, and they got the survivors in line. The rest fell in around them, forming a defensive barrier.

"Let's move out," Leo said, waving a hand at the nearest exit.

CHAPTER 15 - LT. KINGSLEY

"Stick together, guys. Don't get separated," Clare added.

Together, they moved forward at a slow but steady pace, forging a path through the crowd of undead. The fighters gave it their all, protecting the vulnerable within their midst, and Kingsley had never felt prouder. His heart swelled within his chest, and he knew he didn't have to worry about them anymore. *They will be okay. No matter what.*

That knowledge lifted a burden from his shoulders that he hadn't known was there. Using the last of his strength, he helped his people reach the exit. The moment they were through, he placed himself within the opening and yelled, "Run!"

Chris, who was the nearest to him, stopped with a look of confusion on his face. "Lieutenant? What are you doing?"

Kingsley fired a volley of shots at the infected closing in on him, buying himself a little time. Dropping the rifle, he produced a string of grenades from within his jacket and flashed it at Chris. "Get these people out of here. Now!"

"Lieutenant, no!" Chris cried.

Kingsley fixed him with a stern look. "Get out. That's an order."

Chris shook his head. "Why?"

"It's too late for me. Save the others," Kingsley replied, peeling back his sleeve. A crescent bite mark marred the skin on his wrist, leaking droplets of blood.

Chris' expression dropped, and he nodded. "It's been an honor, Sir."

"Same here," Kingsley replied, saluting.

He watched as Chris and the others disappeared into the distance before he turned back. "Godspeed, my friends. Godspeed."

Pulling the pin from one of the grenades, Kingsley threw himself into the crowd and closed the doors behind him. Eager hands reached out to drag him into their midst, but he didn't resist. With a smile, he surrendered to the darkness, knowing it would all be over soon. His death would buy the time his people needed to escape, and that was enough for him. *This is it. This is my purpose. My destiny.*

Chapter 16 - Priya

Priya left George in the company of his friends and continued with her mission. While she felt sorry for him, there were more important things to worry about. Her community was still in danger, and it was her duty to save them.

Dashing through the corridors at top speed, she searched for other survivors. They found a few stumbling around in a haze, looking for a way out. They directed them to the exit, and they soon had a steady trickle of people fleeing the building. But the deeper they went, the harder it became until the only things they encountered were zombies.

After Priya had shot and killed yet another infected, her gun clicked on empty. She paused to reload, and one of her team stepped up and killed the zombie.

Suddenly, a series of violent explosions rocked the building. The walls shook, and chunks of concrete and plaster rained from above.

Priya threw herself to the floor and huddled against the wall, her arms above her head. Dust and mortar filled her nostrils, and her body rocked from side to side.

Finally, the world stopped shaking, and she could look up and take stock. Inspecting her body, she confirmed she was still in one piece. "Everyone okay?"

Scattered replies sounded around her, and she heaved a sigh of relief. "Alright. Get up, and check for injuries."

Everyone did as she asked, and they quickly ascertained they were all fine. "Okay, let's carry on, guys. We still have a mission to complete."

Priya set off down the hallway, but she didn't get far before she encountered an obstacle. A jumble of concrete blocked the way, a direct result of the roof coming down during the explosions. A quick examination was enough to convince her there was no way through, and she had to admit defeat. "It's a no-go, guys. Let's get out of here."

"Is there no way around it?" one of her team members asked.

"It would take too long to find one," Priya said, filled with bitter disappointment. "Whoever is in there is on their own now."

Turning around, she led her team back toward the exit. They ran through the ER and spilled out into the open air. Shivering in the cold wind, they looked around and tried to orient themselves. The lot was in chaos, and they discovered that the evacuation was in full swing.

The gates were open, and the fifty calibers ran at full speed. Guards escorted survivors toward the waiting vehicles, and the first busses were already on their way.

Taking in the situation at a glance, Priya sent her team ahead to help where they could. Before she joined them, she took a moment to catch her breath and sucked in a lungful of the cold air. All she wanted was a single quiet moment to herself.

However, a strange noise made Priya pause, and she turned around to pinpoint the source. What she saw made her blood run cold, and she froze. "What the fuck?"

A horde of zombies advanced from within the hospital,

CHAPTER 16 - PRIYA

shuffling toward her like a tidal wave of rot. They numbered in the dozens, so many she couldn't fathom where they came from. Then it hit her. *They came from above.*

When the roof caved in, it allowed the zombies trapped on the upper levels to invade the bottom floor. *Thank God we didn't stick around, looking for a way past the blockage, or we would've been trapped.*

However, that didn't solve their current problem, and Priya realized she had to do something fast. The horde would spill into the open within minutes, and the evacuation would turn into a massacre. *Shit, shit, shit! What do I do?*

Closing the doors was not an option, thanks to her team's spray of gunfire earlier. The former doors now lay scattered on the ground in a carpet of shattered glass mixed with zombie corpses.

Then she spotted a parked ambulance parked nearby, and an idea popped into her head. Breaking into a run, she sprinted toward the vehicle, reaching it within seconds. She slammed into the side, yanked open the door, and jumped inside. Searching for the keys, she found them in the ignition, a stroke of luck bordering on a miracle. "Yes!"

The engine started without a hitch, another miracle she owed to Coco, and she jammed it into gear. It was a short distance to the ER, and she raced across the space with all the speed she could muster. With a quick turn of the wheel, the ambulance crunched across a field of glass and corpses.

The second she was through the entrance, Priya slammed both feet on the brakes and came to a stop with a squeal of burning rubber.

The ambulance didn't fit inside the opening, and the top and sides scraped against the aluminum frame. While it blocked the doors and trapped the zombies inside, it also left Priya in a sticky situation.

With lightning speed, she assessed her options and realized there was only one way out if she was fast enough.

Jumping out of the vehicle, she dropped to the floor and shimmied underneath the ambulance. The space was narrow, and she had to press her body to the floor while dragging herself along using her hands and elbows.

Behind Priya, the horde drew ever closer, and she expected rabid teeth to fall on her legs at any second. Panic surged through her veins, and she moved as fast as she could manage. *Go, go, go!*

Broken glass cut into her flesh and scraped along her skin. Blood burst from a dozen lacerations, some small and some large, while tiny shards dug into her palms and elbows. Each movement sent flashes of pain throughout her body, but she ignored it and kept going.

When cold fingers grasped her ankle, Priya screamed with terror. She lashed out with her boot and scrambled deeper under the ambulance. Pure adrenalin flushed through her veins and granted her extra speed and strength, a gift from the gods.

Bit by bit, she dragged herself across the ground, ignoring the many rents in her flesh. It was nothing compared to what the undead would do to her should they catch her, and she kept moving no matter what.

It didn't take long to encounter the first corpse. There were dozens of them lying around, shot to ribbons by her team earlier. The smell of rot filled her nose and coated her mouth, so strong she began to gag. Turning her head away, she shouldered past the body and crawled through a pool of

CHAPTER 16 - PRIYA

congealed blood. The cold, sticky liquid squelched with every move she made, and her stomach heaved. *Don't think about it. Just keep moving. You can do it.*

Priya soldiered onward, zigzagging through a minefield of dead zombies, body parts, blood, gunk, and glass. Her breath rasped in and out of her lungs, and sweat burned her eyes. Bile surged up her throat whenever her stomach revolted, and she couldn't see anything in the darkness, but she didn't quit. *Don't stop. Don't stop.*

The words swirled through Priya's head like a mantra, urging her onward until she reached the far end of the vehicle. Helping hands lifted her out from underneath and lifted her up. Gentle fingers examined her injuries while a dozen people swarmed the area and stoppered the gap beneath the ambulance.

Shocked but grateful, Priya stared at the faces of the people helping her. Some were members of her SCERT team, Chris and Matt. Others she recognized from among the firefighter community. Either way, she thanked her lucky stars for being part of such a group and allowed them to lead her to safety.

Behind her, the undead remained trapped inside the hospital, left to beat against the walls with fruitless frustration. Prisoners of their own design, they would have to wait their chance, moldering inside the cages that were their bodies. Ever hungry. Ever yearning for a life that was no longer theirs.

Chapter 17 - Theresa

Theresa stared at the hospital building, her stomach a knot of anxiety. They'd begun the evacuation, opening the gates and letting fully loaded vehicles through the exit. Armed guards kept the infected outside at bay and ensured the safety of everyone on the grounds. Together, they took care of the steady trickle of survivors from within the hospital, and everything went as well as expected.

Then it stopped.

No more survivors.

No more gunshots from within.

Nothing.

"What's going on in there?" Ruby asked.

"Let me try to find out," Theresa said.

She raised the radio to her lips and said, "Lieutenant Kingsley? Are you there? Over."

Nothing sounded but a crackle of static.

"Leo? Priya? Over," she tried again.

More static.

"Is there anyone alive in there at all? Over."

Still nothing.

"Do you think we should send someone in?" Blanca asked, moving closer.

CHAPTER 17 - THERESA

"You should've let me go after Clare," Mason added, his voice thick with recrimination.

"And do what? You're one man alone, and we can't spare more guns," Theresa asked.

"I could've asked George and Amelia. Daisy, too," Mason said.

"George is in no condition to help you, and he needs Amelia by his side," Theresa said.

Mason sighed. "I know."

"As for Daisy, at least she's not moping around like a kid who lost his toy," Theresa added. "She's pitching in like a real trooper."

"Sorry," Mason said.

"Besides, we have to trust Kingsley. The same goes for Leo, Priya, Clare… everyone who's gone inside. They're all fighters, and we have to believe that they can get the job done."

"Let's give them more time," Ruby agreed. "I hope there are more survivors. So many are still missing."

"I know," Theresa said, chewing on a thumbnail.

Suddenly, a terrific blast rocked the night. Windows exploded outward in a spray of glass, and a group of survivors burst through the main entrance. They were led by Leo and Clare, with more bringing up the rear.

"Leo! Clare! You're alive," Theresa cried, ready to cry with relief. "What happened in there? I heard an explosion."

"I'm not sure," Clare said, looking confused.

"Me neither," Leo said.

Two men stepped forward. They were part of Kingsley's SCERT team, Chris and Matt. "It was Kingsley. He set off a grenade blast."

"But why?" Theresa asked.

"He was infected and wanted to buy us more time," Chris answered.

"No! I'm so sorry," Clare said. "He was right there. I thought he followed us out."

"He was a good leader and an even better man," Chris said, his expression stark. Then he looked around. "Where's Priya?"

"Still inside," Theresa said.

"Shit," Chris said, turning around.

He and Matt ran toward the hospital, and Theresa let them go. She had her own problems to deal with. The flood of survivors from the hospital were in a panic. They pushed and shoved each other out of the way to get onto the waiting vehicles, ignoring any efforts to examine them. Yelling orders, Theresa tried to maintain control of the situation, but it was nearly impossible. "People, please. Queue over here!"

Finally, Blanca released several warning shots and spoke through her loudspeaker. "Listen up, everyone. No one is getting onto a bus without following the proper procedure. Got it? And if you try to skip it, I will shoot you myself."

The crowd froze, looking around with wide-eyed terror, and Theresa took the opportunity to step in. "Form a line right there and let one of the volunteers check you for injuries. Afterward, you will be directed to a waiting vehicle for evacuation."

No one seemed happy with the instructions, but they obeyed, not wanting to attract Blanca's attention. Jakes, Ruby, Susan, and Theresa worked as fast as they could, separating the infected from the healthy. Everyone got onto a vehicle, accompanied by a driver and an armed guard.

Once a vehicle was full, Theresa gave the all-clear, and it moved to the head of the convoy. Guards operating the gates

CHAPTER 17 - THERESA

let them through, and they drove toward the temporary safe house.

Halfway through, Chris and Matt returned with Priya. The woman looked like she'd been dragged backward through a bush, and she was covered in blood but still alive. "There are hundreds more infected inside. You'd better get everyone out now. I don't know how long the barriers can hold," Priya said, bleeding from a dozen cuts.

"How's that possible?"

"The explosion caved in the roof, opening a way for them to get in from the other floors."

"Alright. Let's get a move on," Theresa said, waving people on.

She quickly checked Priya for signs of infection and found none, though it was hard to say with all her injuries.

"It's okay. I'll go with the quarantine bus," Priya said.

"Me too," Chris said.

"And me," Matt added.

"We'll make sure they don't turn on anyone," Priya added.

"Okay, thank you!" Theresa said, pointing to the quarantine vehicle.

Before Priya got on, she asked, "What about George? Is he okay?"

"He's fine and on his way to the safe house," Theresa said.

"Good," Priya said, looking relieved.

She left, followed by Chris and Matt.

Theresa returned to her job and came face to face with Sandi. The young teacher looked frightened, but she had Paisley in one hand and a young boy in the other. "Theresa! I'm so glad to see you."

"And I am just as happy to see you all safe and sound," Theresa replied, sending up a prayer of thanks.

After that, she spotted several more familiar faces. Madeleine Koch, the head matron. Lindsey, Dirk, and Stella, all of them from the hospital board.

"Have you seen Sophia?" Lindsey asked.

"Or Dr. Bond?" Madeleine asked.

"No, I'm sorry, but I haven't seen any of them," Theresa said, shaking her head.

Madeleine burst into tears, and Theresa felt sorry for the woman. They'd all lost people that day. Some more than others, but there was no time for grieving. They had work to do.

Finally, the last full vehicle exited the grounds, leaving only a handful of people behind. Theresa studied them, noting how exhausted they looked. They were holding on by a thread, barely keeping it together.

"Alright, guys. This is it. We are the last. Thank you for doing everything you could to ensure the safety of our community, and may you be blessed for your efforts. There is nothing left for us now but to get ourselves to safety. Let's go!"

One by one, they climbed into the last remaining vehicles, the fire trucks from the old station. Blanca had already left, driving the quarantine bus, but the last of the guards quickly piled in. The two fifty-calibers rode on the back of a truck, safe from enemy hands, along with everything else that could be scrounged up from the grounds.

Within minutes, the Virtua Willingboro Hospital and its community were no more. Nothing remained but an empty graveyard filled with the corpses of the dead and the living dead. A bloated carcass left rotting in the sun for the vultures to pick over, and vultures there would be. Whoever brought about its fall would be back, ready to profit from its demise,

CHAPTER 17 - THERESA

and Theresa was determined to find out who it was.

Chapter 18 - Zoey

Zoey huddled in the far corner of the room, hidden in the shadows. It was the safest place for her, away from Blackwell and his men. She didn't trust the leader's promise that she and Banks would be treated well. She didn't trust him or his people to protect a rock. They were all murderers and thieves—parasites who preyed on others.

Her eyes panned the room, searching for signs of danger. It was impossible to relax when surrounded by a bunch of killers. Blackwell was still on the roof, basking in the glory of his triumph over the hospital community, but that didn't mean she could afford to let her guard down.

Besides Blackwell, there were six more of them, including Lucien. He was missing too, gone to sabotage the hospital and let the dead out of the morgue. *I hope he gets caught, the asshole. I hope he's lying in a ditch somewhere with his throat slit, bleeding out while zombies feast on his entrails.*

She closed her eyes, imagining every detail of his suffering. For a moment, it was sweet bliss until a commotion at the entrance spoiled her fun.

Craning her head, Zoey spotted a blood-spattered Lucien walking into the room, followed by two accomplices. They looked very satisfied with themselves, and her blood boiled.

CHAPTER 18 - ZOEY

Her broken fingers and ribs twinged at the sight of Lucien's face, and she vividly remembered how he'd tortured her. Hate burned within her chest like acid, and she itched to throw herself at him. *I bet I could wipe that smug smile off his face.*

As if Banks knew what she was thinking, he sidled closer. "Don't. They'll kill you."

"Who cares? I'm dead anyway."

"There are worse things than death," Banks said with a look of sorrow.

Zoey favored him with an evil look. "Go away, Banks. You're just as bad as they are."

"No, I'm not. I'm still me. I'm still Banks," he said. "Please, try to understand. I had to do it."

"No, you didn't. You're a traitor," Zoey replied, looking away.

"I had no choice," Banks replied. "They were going to kill you. They were torturing you."

"You should've let them," Zoey replied, refusing to meet his gaze.

"I couldn't," Banks replied. "I love you, Zoey. I have loved you for a long time."

Zoey's breath hitched in her throat. Those words might have meant something special to her at one time, but now they filled her with nothing but scorn. When Banks tentatively reached for her injured hand, she pulled away with a hiss. "Don't touch me, you monster."

Banks stared at her for a few seconds before he got up and fetched the med kit. "Let me check your injuries."

"Fuck off, Banks. I'm fine."

"Stop being stubborn. You're not fine. I can see you're in pain."

"Leave me alone."

"At least let me do this for you. You know you need my help," Banks insisted.

"Fine," Zoey replied. "But don't think this changes anything."

"I know," Banks said, looking miserable.

He opened the med kit and checked her ribs. Two were broken, making it hard to breathe. Three of her fingers were fractured, but they didn't bother her nearly as much as the gunshot wound in her shoulder.

She found it hard to look at him while he worked to strap, bandage, and disinfect her wounds. Finally, he gave her painkillers, a bottle of water, and a protein bar. "You have to keep up your strength."

During the entire procedure, she glared at him, hating every single anatomy of his being. Everything about him put her off. Every feature that she'd loved before now filled her with disgust. But she knew he spoke the truth, and she reluctantly took the pills, drank the water, and ate the food. Afterward, she felt better, and she even dozed off for a few minutes.

Suddenly, Blackwell stormed down from the roof, furious. He immediately targeted Lucien, shouting, "What the fuck was that?"

"What do you mean?" Lucien asked, clearly confused.

"Most of them are supposed to be dead. Why are so many survivors leaving the grounds? And what the hell was that explosion?"

"Sorry, Boss. I don't know about any explosion," Lucien replied.

"You don't?" Blackwell asked with deceptive stillness.

"No, Bo—"

Blackwell lashed out with a punch, landing a direct hit to the face. Blood spurted from Lucien's broken nose and dribbled down the front of his shirt, adding to the gore already there.

"This was not how it was supposed to go," Blackwell bellowed. "I wanted most of them dead. Dead!"

"I know, Boss," Lucien replied.

"Shut the fuck up," Blackwell said, his face the color of beetroot. A vein throbbed in his temple, and he looked like he was going to have a heart attack. "That explosion just took out half of the building. My building. My supplies. Mine, mine, mine!" He paced up and down like a caged lion. "And now, I'll have to deal with dozens of pissed-off survivors plotting to put my head on a stake."

Lucien hung his head, looking contrite. "Sorry, Boss."

Zoey smiled, happy to see him suffer. It was the first time she'd seen him look anything but arrogant and self-assured. Now he looked a little like she felt. Scared. *Fucker.*

Lucien shot her a baleful glare. "This is your fault."

Banks stepped in between her and Blackwell. "No, it wasn't. She had no way of knowing what would happen."

"She could've warned us. So could he," Lucien said, pointing at her and Banks.

"That's ridiculous," Zoey burst out, unable to keep her mouth shut. "There was no way in hell we could've predicted any of this."

Lucien snarled at her with bared teeth, "Don't talk to me like that, woman."

"I'll say it because it's true," Zoey insisted.

"Zoey, please," Banks whispered.

"Leave me alone," Zoey said. "I don't talk to traitors."

"Ouch, that must've hurt," Blackwell said, bursting out into sudden laughter.

Zoey glared at him and wished the earth would swallow her

whole. All eyes were on her, and the room spun as everyone mocked her. Shifting in her seat, she wished she could teleport herself to any place but there.

With a swift change of mood, Blackwell turned to Lucien. "Wash that crap off your face and meet me on the roof. We have much to discuss."

"Yes, Boss," Lucien replied, hurrying to obey.

Blackwell threw her and Banks a mean look. "You two stay right here. If you cause any trouble, you're dead."

"You said you'd treat us well," Banks protested. "We gave up everything for you."

"You did it because you had no choice," Blackwell said. "There's a difference."

"You promised," Banks insisted.

Blackwell's face reddened, and he stormed toward Banks. "Don't you dare tell me what to do. Now sit down and shut up until I get back."

With those parting words, Blackwell left, followed by Lucien and a couple of others. The rest stayed behind, leering at Banks and Zoey.

A stricken Banks turned to Zoey and said, "I'm sorry I got you into this. I never should've taken you with me on that run."

For the first time, Zoey felt a twinge of sympathy for him. "You couldn't have known."

"No, but I was always dragging you everywhere because I wanted you for myself. I was greedy, and now we're both paying the price."

Zoey stared at her hands, picking at the bandages around her fingers. Banks' admission came as a surprise, but some part of her had always known. "The funny thing is, if you'd told me, I could've loved you back."

CHAPTER 18 - ZOEY

"And now, it's too late," Banks asked.

"Yes," Zoey said, not meeting his gaze.

"I know you'll never forgive me, but at least try to understand why I did what I did," Banks said. "You were suffering, Zoey. You were in so much pain, and I couldn't stand it. I still can't."

"I get it, Banks," Zoey said, "but I'm not a child. Some weakling that you have to protect. It was my choice to make. Die under torture to protect our people or cut a deal to save our own hides. You took that decision for me."

"Could you have watched while they tortured me?" Banks asked.

"I don't know. Maybe not, but I would've tried to give you a say in your future," Zoey said with a shrug. "Now, everyone we know is dead, we are traitors, and we're stuck with these murderers."

"You're not the traitor. I am," Banks said.

"What does it matter? We're stuck here," Zoey said. "How long do you think Blackwell's supposed protection will last? Look at them. They're staring at me like I'm a piece of prime rib, and they're starving."

"I'll protect you," Banks said.

"That's just it," Zoey said. "You can't protect me because you've got no leverage. You lost that the moment you gave up our people."

Banks stared at her, his face pale. "I'll get you out of this. I swear it."

"How?"

"Don't worry about it. When the time comes, run, and don't look back. Go to the safe house," Banks said.

Zoey frowned. "Don't do anything stupid, Banks."

"It's too late. I already did," Banks said.

Banks turned away from her, and Zoey was left to chew on her nails while worry churned in her gut. Whatever he had planned, it meant someone's death. The question was, for who?

Chapter 19 - Nikki

Nikki drove throughout the day and into the afternoon. She avoided the houses she saw by the side of the road and bypassed any small towns. The last thing she wanted was another zombie encounter, and she didn't trust people that much either. Choosing the back roads made it easier, and she didn't come across many individuals except for the occasional car.

The first time it happened, Nikki spotted a blue sedan ahead. The car drove slowly, well below the speed limit. Swallowing hard, she edged closer to the vehicle, one hand resting on her gun. The reason for the car's slow pace soon became evident. It was loaded to the brim with a small family and their belongings. Trunks and suitcases balanced on the roof, swaying from side to side.

Nikki was stuck behind the car for several miles, unsure what to do. She edged to the side and caught a glimpse of a frightened face in the side mirror. Slowing down, she backed off, but the situation grew tenser with each passing moment.

"I can't sit behind you all day," Nikki mumbled, growing impatient.

Gearing down, Nikki sped up and overtook the blue sedan. As she drove past, she looked to the side and locked eyes with the driver.

He looked every bit as scared as she felt. Unsure and uncertain. They stared at each other for a second, each recognizing a little of themselves in the other person.

Finally, Nikki nodded.

The driver nodded back, and the lady beside him offered a tiny wave. Three children in the back stared at her with owlish eyes: two boys and a girl.

Nikki waved back, and Cooper barked. The kids smiled. It was sweet. Normal. Then the moment was over, and Nikki left them in her wake.

An hour later, she was still thinking about that family. It was hard not to worry about them. Parents and three kids in an overloaded sedan? The odds were stacked against them.

"Forget it, Nikki. You can't care about them. You have to look after yourself and Cooper."

Cooper gazed at her with his big brown eyes, causing a twinge of guilt to stir within her chest.

"What?" Nikki said, looking away. "I can't help them. You know I can't."

Cooper whined and looked away.

"Fine, be mad at me, but there's nothing I can do for them. They're on their own." Nikki shook her head and focused on the road ahead.

The second time she passed a car, it was easier. The third and fourth times even more so.

"See, Cooper? We're not the only people on the road, and we can't worry about all of them."

Cooper ignored her, his gaze fixed on the passing countryside. "What? Not talking to me now?"

Cooper whined, one paw scratching at the door.

Nikki frowned. "Do you want to pee? Is that it?"

CHAPTER 19 - NIKKI

Cooper whined again, and she decided to pull over. "Time for a break!"

She found an empty spot by the side of the road and guided the truck onto it. Killing the engine, she got out and opened the door for the dog. Cooper rushed past her, almost knocking her off her feet in his haste to reach a patch of grass. The moment he could, he squatted and did his business with a look of extreme relief, much to Nikki's amusement.

"Haha, you go ahead, boy," Nikki said, rummaging in the back of the truck for a snack.

She poured a bowl of water for the dog and grabbed a packet of nuts and a cold drink. Leaning against the side of the truck, she chewed on the peanuts with relish before washing them down with the lukewarm drink. "Ugh, I miss refrigeration and ice."

Cooper showed up moments later, barking and wagging his tail.

"Much better, huh?" Nikki teased.

Cooper yipped.

"My turn, okay?" Nikki said. "Keep watch."

Making her way to the bushes, she did her business. Afterward, she wiped with the supply of toilet paper she'd grabbed from the gas station, washed her hands, and covered the mess with branches. "Ugh. Now I really miss plumbing. Toilets. Showers. Running water."

With a sigh of regret for comforts lost, Nikki made her way back to the truck. "Come on, Cooper. Time to go."

Cooper ignored her, running around the clearing instead. He peed on bushes, sniffed wildflowers, and barked at the birds in the trees.

Watching him, Nikki was tempted to linger. Being stuck in

a truck all day wasn't fun, and Cooper needed the exercise, but she couldn't afford to stay. Not when zombies might be in the area.

"Come on, boy. Please," Nikki pleaded. "It's not safe out here." Raising her voice, she yelled. "Come on!"

Cooper stopped running and slunk over to her with his tail between his legs. With droopy ears, he jumped into the truck and lay down.

"I'm sorry, boy. I don't mean to be hard on you. I promise we'll stop again soon, and you can run around as much as you want."

Cooper didn't bother to look at her, and she felt terrible for spoiling his fun. Starting the engine, she drove away with a sense of regret. However, they hadn't gone far when dark clouds closed in on the horizon. Thunder rumbled in the distance, rattling the windows in their frames. A crack of lightning caused her to jump, and Cooper barked with fright. "Holy crap, that was a big one."

Clutching the wheel, Nikki pushed onward, hoping the storm would blow over, but no such luck. A couple of miles further, fat raindrops plopped onto the windscreen, and she switched on the lights and the wipers. It grew darker, the sky blackening with threads of silver running through the clouds.

As the rain came down harder and harder, it became impossible to see, and she had no choice but to pull over. "Well, boy. I guess we'll have to sit this one out."

Cooper whined, huddled into a tiny ball on the seat. He didn't like the storm either and sought her protection with a nudge of his nose.

"It will be alright, boy. Don't worry," Nikki said, steering the truck off the road and into the shelter of a stand of trees.

CHAPTER 19 - NIKKI

Opening both windows a crack for fresh air, Nikki removed a jacket from her backpack in the footwell and put it on. Next, she untied the blanket roll tied to the bottom and draped it over her and Cooper.

"Come on, boy. Cuddle up. The storm will blow over in no time. Promise."

Cooper obeyed, tucking his body in next to her. She wrapped her arms around him, and they snuggled on the seat.

It felt safe in their nest, tucked away from the storm. The trees formed a green canopy overhead and warded off the worst of the rain. Thunder rumbled overhead, and lightning struck in the distance, but it seemed far away and unreal.

It didn't take long for them to doze off, but Nikki woke up occasionally to take a few sips of water. She also let them both out for a quick stretch of the legs. However, they were eager to get out of the cold and wet and wasted no time returning to their snug little den. Afternoon faded into dusk. The rain stopped, the clouds cleared, and the moon began its rise on the far horizon.

Nikki stirred underneath the blanket and blinked at their surroundings. A cramp had formed in her right calf, and she winced with pain when she tried to move. Stretching it out, she straightened her leg and considered their options. "Are you awake, boy?"

Cooper blinked at her with lazy eyes but didn't bother to move.

Nikki stifled a grin. "That comfy, huh? Aren't you hungry? Don't you want to pee?"

Cooper yawned in reply before tucking his nose back underneath the blanket.

"I get it. I don't want to go out into the cold either," Nikki said, but her stomach cramped with hunger. "I'll make it quick."

After carefully looking around, she cracked open the door, gun in hand. Calling out, she listened for movement. "Anything out there?"

When nothing stirred, she climbed out and removed a corner of the tarp covering her supplies. She was glad she'd thought of it, or her stuff would've been soaked. Removing a couple of cans, a bottle of water, a chocolate bar, and Cooper's bowls, she replaced the tarp and hurried back to the cab.

Although it was cramped, she preferred feeding the dog inside the truck. It was rapidly growing dark, and she couldn't see much in the gathering gloom. The moon was a mere sliver in the sky, and the last of the sun's golden light winked out below the treeline.

Once Cooper had eaten and drunk his fill, she let him out to relieve himself while she stood watch with the gun. Thankfully, he kept it quick.

Next, it was her turn, and she relieved herself next to the truck. Jumping back inside, she ate her can of sardines and washed it down with some water.

Afterward, she turned to Cooper. "What do you say, boy? Do we push on, or do we spend the night here? It's super cramped, but there's no guarantee we'll find anything better on the road ahead."

Cooper responded by curling up on the seat and closing his eyes with a deep huff, and Nikki gave in with a smile. "Guess we're staying right here."

Making herself as comfortable as possible, she settled in for the night. What followed was a long period during which she tossed and turned, unable to settle down. The utter darkness and silence bothered her, and she kept imagining zombies

CHAPTER 19 - NIKKI

emerging from the trees to surround the truck.

It was almost dawn when she finally fell into a deep sleep, worn out by the stress and strain. Sometime later, she woke to birds chirping in the trees. Bright light streamed into the cab, and she sat upright with a groan. Every muscle in her body ached, stuck too long in one position. "Oh, man, that hurts."

Cooper blinked at her from his spot in the footwell, and she patted him on the head. "Good morning, sleepyhead."

After a solid stretch and a big yawn, Nikki sat upright and surveyed the area around the truck. The clearing was empty, with no signs of anything living or dead, and she opened the door for Cooper. "Feel like a run, boy?"

Cooper's tail wagged in agreement, and she let him out of the cab. With joyous abandon, he ran around the open area, barking and sniffing at anything that caught his attention: Birds, bees, butterflies, and spiders alike. He chased them all.

Nikki watched for a few minutes, a smile on her face. It was good to see the dog so happy, and she allowed him to run amok while she readied a bowl of food and water for breakfast. Once he'd drunk and eaten, she turned her attention to herself. A granola bar and orange juice filled the hollow in her stomach, and she rinsed and packed away the dishes.

A quick study of the map showed her that Burlington wasn't far. They could reach it before the end of the day if they didn't run into trouble and had enough fuel. Checking the tank, she noticed it was low and filled up using both jerry cans. "That should do it. The last thing I want is to visit another zombie-infested gas station."

Memories of the last stop caused her to shudder. It had been a narrow escape, and those fresh zoms had almost punched her ticket. She did miss the security of sleeping in a building and the fact that she'd had a proper bathroom with running water. Out in the country, there wasn't much she could do in the way of ablutions, but a handful of wet wipes got rid of the worst dirt and sweat. She also combed her hair, washed her face, brushed her teeth, and pulled on a clean t-shirt.

"Guess that'll have to do," Nikki said, packing her stuff. She allowed Cooper a few more minutes of freedom before she called him back, and he flew into the cab with a happy look. "Ready to go, boy?"

His tail wagged, and she soon got them back on the road. Fresh air streamed through the windows, smelling of damp earth and rain. It felt good to be alive, and she allowed a sliver of optimism to creep into her heart.

Several miles later, she spotted a car parked by the side of the road. Slowing down, she recognized the blue sedan she'd seen the day before. It must've passed her while she waited out the storm, or they'd driven through the night.

Either way, it didn't look like they were going much further. Not by car, anyway. The father stood beside the vehicle with a defeated look and an empty jerry can by his feet. They were out of gas.

Slowing down, Nikki debated her options. On the one hand, she wanted to help but had no fuel to spare. She only had enough to get her to Burlington. No further. As much as she wanted to share, she couldn't.

Speeding up, she attempted to drive past, but the father had different ideas. Jumping into the road, he forced her to stop. "Help! Help, please!"

Nikki stopped the truck in the middle of the road and rolled down her window. Her stomach churned when she spoke the dreaded words. "I'm sorry, but I can't help you."

"Please," the man pleaded. "We're out of gas, and the next town is still far away. Too far to walk."

"I'm sorry, but I don't have any gas to spare," Nikki said, feeling like shit when she said it. "I only have enough to get to where I'm going."

"You must have a little?" the man asked, raising his voice. "We don't need much. Just a gallon or two."

"A gallon or two won't be enough to get you to the next town," Nikki said.

"Maybe not, but it'll get us closer," the man hedged.

"I'm sorry, but no," Nikki said, growing uncomfortable. Sensing her emotions, Cooper growled at the man, and she reached over to restrain him. "No, Cooper. Be quiet, please. I'll handle this."

Cooper obeyed, but he didn't look happy about it, and Nikki glanced at the car with the wife and kids sitting inside. They looked scared, and she didn't blame them, but she couldn't allow their plight to sway her. *I have to look after myself and Cooper first.*

"Please don't make me say it again. I can't give you any fuel," Nikki repeated, praying he'd listen.

"If you leave us here, we'll die," the man said, edging toward her car. "We don't have a lot of food and water, and the kids can't walk that far. Especially out in the open with those things around."

"I could give you a lift into town?" Nikki offered. "You could get an extra car with more gas and come back for your family?"

"I can't leave them out here alone," the man protested. "What if something happens to them?"

"I'm sure they'll be fine. They can stay in the car, and it won't be long," Nikki said. "I'll even give them extra food and water if you're worried about that."

"I can't take that chance. They're all I have. Please, I'm only asking for a little bit of gas," the man said.

Nikki shook her head. She felt like a piece of shit, but she had to stick to her guns. "I'm sorry, but no. A lift is all I can offer. Take it or leave it."

"Can't you take all of us?" the man asked. "We won't be any trouble."

Nikki thought it over, but she didn't like the idea of so many strangers in her car. It was too dangerous, and they could overwhelm her within seconds. She also didn't like how the man moved closer to her car. Too close for comfort. "I'll take one of you. No more."

"I'm afraid that's not good enough," the man said, his expression changing from desperate to calculating.

Nikki stiffened in her seat and reached for the gun at her side, ready for a fight. "Don't come any closer."

"Why? What are you going to do? Run me over in front of my kids?" the man asked. "All I'm asking for is a bit of help. Are you that heartless?"

Nikki's eyes narrowed, and anger flared in her chest. She recognized the signs of manipulation from a mile away. Rex had been a master manipulator, and nothing was more guaranteed to piss her off than someone doing it to her. "Listen, mister. I'm not giving you any of my gas, only a lift. Take it or leave it."

The man hesitated, looking from his family to her. Finally, he stepped aside and waved at her to pass. "I can't leave them out here alone. Go."

"I'm sorry," Nikki said, relaxing somewhat. "But I'll make

CHAPTER 19 - NIKKI

you a promise."

"What's that?" the man asked.

"If I can find a safe place to refuel up ahead, I'll circle back and bring you some gas," Nikki said.

"Thank you. I'd appreciate that," the man said.

Shifting into gear, Nikki drove past the man, carefully keeping an eye on him. She still didn't trust him and wanted nothing more than to leave him and his family behind, no matter how sorry she felt for them. As their eyes drew level, she managed a curt nod of sympathy, thankful that the tense encounter was over. "Good luck."

Suddenly, the man's hand became a blur. He pulled something from the back of his pants and aimed it at her—a gun. "Get out of the car! Now!"

Nikki reacted instantly to the threat, jamming her foot onto the gas. There was not a snowflake's chance in hell she'd stop, only to be shot or abandoned by the side of the road with nothing. Either option meant death.

The truck's engine roared, and the tires squealed as she raced from the scene. The man yelled something incoherent and fired off several shots. One clipped the side mirror, shattering the glass. Two more hit the body, cutting through the steelwork like a hot knife through butter. Another whizzed by the open window, so close she could hear the whine of its trajectory.

"Oh, shit!" Nikki yelled, ducking down.

The truck swerved across the road, heading straight for the trees, and she yanked the steering wheel to the side. Zigzagging across the asphalt, she fought for control of the vehicle, and Cooper yelped as he was thrown from side to side like a rag doll.

Another bullet clipped the door frame, and a shard of metal

pegged into the soft flesh of her cheek. Hot blood ran down her face and dripped onto her shirt, but she hardly felt a thing. Adrenalin coursed through her veins, and her entire focus lay on the road again. Escape was all that mattered. Everything else was secondary.

Nikki clutched the wheel with both hands and managed to straighten the truck. She changed gears and hit the gas, desperate to escape the hail of bullets. The vehicle sped up, and the blue sedan and its occupants faded into the distance.

Sagging with relief, Nikki unclenched her hands from the wheel and took stock of the situation. Her fingers were stiff, blood ran unchecked from the wound in her cheek, and Cooper was howling with fright.

"It's okay, boy. It's alright. You can calm down now. It's over," Nikki said, reaching out with one shaky hand. She patted the dog's head, running her hand over his golden fur in a soothing rhythm. "There you go. See? We're safe."

Finally, Cooper stopped crying and lay down on the seat with a whimper. It hurt to see him so upset, and her heart ached for him. The poor dog had been through a lot, and its nerves were shot. For good reasons, too. First, he lost his owner to the infection, then his zombified owner tried to eat him. He found a new friend in Nikki, but so far, they'd run into trouble around every corner, barely escaping with their lives. "I'm sorry, Cooper. I'm not doing a very good job of looking after you, am I?"

Suddenly, her entire body began to shake. Her teeth chattered, and her head felt woozy. The spurt of adrenalin that had kept her going disappeared in a rush, leaving her drained and exhausted. Tears welled up, and she had no choice but to pull over.

CHAPTER 19 - NIKKI

Grinding to a halt, Nikki killed the engine and stared into the distance. Delayed shock flooded her brain, and she burst into tears. "We almost died, Cooper."

Cooper whined and crept closer, laying his head on her lap. She wrapped her arms around him, sobbing in earnest. "It's my fault. I shouldn't have stopped. I shouldn't have trusted that man."

Shaking her head, Nikki thought back to the previous day. To the first time she'd seen the father and his family. They'd looked so ordinary. Who'd have thought the father was capable of such violence? "He could have killed me. He would have killed me."

Then she remembered the desperation in the man's eyes and realized she couldn't blame him. He was looking out for his family. Whatever that meant. *Just like I look out for Cooper. I'd do anything for him. He's my family now.*

Holding onto Cooper's comforting warmth, the shock faded until she was herself again. Sitting upright, she wiped away the tears and smiled at her furry friend. "Are you ready to go, boy? Feeling better?"

Cooper licked her hand in response, and she gave him a final hug. "Alrighty, then. Burlington, here we come!"

Nikki started the truck's engine, looked around, and pulled away. With both hands firmly on the wheel, she resumed her quest to find her brother, George, and this time, she didn't look back.

Chapter 20 - Mason

Mason quickly set up a perimeter at the safe house and secured the property. Blanca, Priya, Matt, and Chris helped him. They were more familiar with the location, and they knew all of the remaining guards. Together, they cleared any infected in the area, parked the vehicles, moved everyone inside, and set up a patrol roster.

Inside the abandoned office block, Theresa took charge, aided by a small group of volunteers. The first thing they did was check the supplies. There wasn't much: A few crates containing hospital-issue blankets, sheets, and scrubs. Pallets of bottled water. Cases of canned soup. Boxes filled with basic cutlery. A couple of propane camping stoves and an extensive first-aid kit.

Working fast, Theresa and her crew divided the survivors between the available rooms and equipped each person with a blanket and water bottle. Those needing clothes had to make do with scrubs, and the sheets were ripped up for bandages. Susan and Lindsey set up a makeshift kitchen, warmed up the canned soup, and handed out bowls to everyone while Ruby and Ellen treated their injuries.

Those who were infected were likewise treated for their injuries, given food and water, and separated into rooms with

CHAPTER 20 - MASON

either family, friends, or a minder for company. For the moment, their fate hung in the balance.

Afterward, Mason convened a meeting, ready to discuss their next steps. Looking around the small room, he broached the subject. "As you all know, we've lost our home, and we are on the run from enemies unknown. I called you here to discuss our next move and to decide who will take which role in the coming days. With Lieutenant Kingsley and Sophia Ward gone, someone else must step up to the plate. Does anyone know how many people we've lost?"

"We do not have an exact count yet, but I can tell you this much," Theresa said. "Sophia Ward, Dr. Bond, Lieutenant Kingsley, and Stella from the Hospital Board are dead, along with a third of the original hospital community. When it comes to the firefighters, we lost Bobbi. Losses among the original school survivors number roughly half, along with Claudia and James."

"Only one loss among the firefighters?" Priya said with an arched eyebrow. "You got off lightly."

"We only got off because Bobbi knew something was up and warned our people. Most of us were able to make it out before it all went to hell," Theresa replied, her tone sharp.

"Of course. I didn't mean to imply anything," Priya said, hanging her head.

"We need to figure out what to do with all of these people," Theresa said. "The city is not safe."

"What about Burlington Island?" Clare asked. "It's big enough for all of us, about a mile long, has a lake for water, and we can fish for food."

"What about infected? It's in the middle of the city," Mason said.

"It's also in the middle of the Delaware River, and there are only two access points: The promenade that runs to the Burlington Bristol bridge and the deer crossover on the island's northern side. With a little luck, we can throw up some quick defenses and barricades."

"That's not a bad idea," Priya said. "We can use the fifty-caliber guns to create choke points in case a horde tries to invade. Or if more bad guys show up to take what we have."

"And there are small sheds and houses on the northern end of the island," Clare said, warming to her subject. "We can use those to create a home."

"I think there used to be an amusement park once," Theresa mused. "And there's a boat yard across from the island in Burlington with docks, gas pumps, and a repair shop. That would be very useful."

"What are the alternatives?" Clare asked. "Leave the city? We don't know what's out there. Staying here? It's too dangerous, and we need space for crops. We need water. The island gives us all of that."

"What about a farm?" Sarah asked. "Like the one Timothy's dad lives on. It's outside the city, isn't it?"

"Yes, but it's a long drive with a lot of people," Timothy said. "Plus, my dad could never take in so many extra mouths to feed."

"Aren't there empty farms we could use?" Sarah asked.

"Maybe, but none close to my dad. The farmers there have formed a network with a militia, and they all look after each other. A bunch of city people would not be welcomed."

"I see," Sarah said, looking disappointed.

"He might be willing to trade," Timothy said. "If you could set up a community on the island, my dad might be open to

CHAPTER 20 - MASON

negotiations."

"What would we offer, though?" Theresa asked.

"We'll have access to the city," Clare said. "I know supply runs are dangerous, but if we plan them carefully, we could have a lot to offer."

"That's true," Theresa said, looking thoughtful.

"Alright. This island business seems like the best idea we've had so far. Who's in?" Mason asked. One by one, people raised their hands or nodded their heads in agreement. "Then it's settled. We're moving to the island."

"Except me," Timothy said. "I need to go see my dad."

"I'm going with you," George said, surprising everyone.

"George?" Mason asked.

"I want to go with Timothy. We can stay there for a while, helping out and setting up a trade agreement with the other farmers. Once the Island community is ready, we can broker our first trade."

"And you want to do this?" Mason asked.

"I need a change from all of this," George said. "Besides, Sebastian needs a real home. Not some dingy office block in the middle of a zombie-infested city. I owe Bobbi that much."

"Alright. When do you want to leave?" Mason asked.

"As soon as possible," Timothy said. "The sooner we get there, the better."

"Well, you can take one of the smaller vehicles," Priya said. "There's a Jeep that can handle tough terrain, and we can spare supplies for the trip."

"Good, then we leave first thing in the morning," George said.

"And the rest of us will move to the second safe house, grab everything we can, and relocate to the island," Mason said.

"Not all of us," Amelia objected.

"Why not?" Mason asked.

"Some of us have to stay behind, find out who did this to us, and kill them all," Amelia said.

Mason stared at her, taken aback. "What?"

"You heard me. This wasn't an accident. Someone let those things out," Amelia argued.

"She's right," Priya piped in. "Someone killed three of our watch guards. We found the bodies during the evacuation. Their throats were slit. That's no accident."

"But how would they know about the morgue? The undead?" Mason asked.

"There's still the question of the missing Banks and Zoey," Priya said. "I suspect they were kidnapped and questioned."

"Questioned?" Clare said, her face pale.

"More like tortured," Mason added.

Silence fell across the group as each absorbed his words. They invoked a sense of horror unique to the word torture.

Clare shuddered. "If that's true, we have to rescue them."

"If there's anything left to rescue," Mason said.

"We can't," Priya said. "At least not until we know where they are. Until then, they're on their own."

"But do we want to do this?" Mason asked. "Do we want to start a war we might not win?"

"The war has already begun, and they fired the first shot," Amelia said. "Besides, they'll come after us again if we don't stop them now."

"She's right," Blanca said. "These people are killers. To them, we are lambs for the slaughter. We need to show them we are wolves."

Mason sucked in a deep breath, his heart heavy at the

CHAPTER 20 - MASON

prospect of war. But Blanca and Amelia each had a point. If they didn't fight now, they'd be sitting ducks later. "Alright, but this is strictly volunteer only. Who wants to stay?"

"I'm staying," Amelia said. "Daisy too."

"We'll stay," Chris said, indicating himself and Matt. "They killed Kingsley."

"We'll stay, as well," Ellen said, holding onto Rick's hand. "You'll need someone with medical experience, and I learned a lot at the hospital."

"I'm staying too," Mike said, followed by Leo.

"Me too," Blanca said, her expression cold.

"No," Priya said. "You must go to the island. They'll need someone with experience and authority to handle the guards and keep everyone safe."

"Why can't you do it?" Blanca asked.

"I would, but I have a different road to take," Priya said.

Blanca stared at her for a while before she shrugged. "Fine. You are still second-in-command next to Kingsley, and I will follow your lead."

"Thank you," Priya said. "But once you are on the island, you are in command. All I ask is that you keep our people safe and work with their chosen leaders."

"Alright, I can do that," Blanca said.

"Good. Eight people are enough," Frank said. "You must be able to move, strike, and escape before your enemy knows you are there. Plus, the fewer you are, the less noise you'll make, and the less you'll need to survive."

"Good advice," Mason said.

"But they'll need a leader," Frank added, throwing Mason a pointed look.

"Me?" Mason asked.

"Yes, you," Frank said.

"I can do it," Clare said. "I want to."

"You are too impulsive. This mission needs someone who can take a step back. Someone with a cooler head than yours."

Clare opened her mouth as if to protest but quickly closed it again. "Damn. Frank is right."

"Of course I am. The best place for you is on the island," Frank said. "It will be hard, back-breaking work and require strong people like you to drive the rest along."

"You mean, crack the whip?" Clare asked.

"Exactly," Frank said.

With a sigh, Clare gave in. "Fine. I'll go to the island."

"And I'll stay, I guess," Mason conceded.

"Good," Frank said, with more than a hint of smugness.

Mason resisted the urge to roll his eyes. "On to the next piece of business. What do we do about the infected in our midst?"

"We separated them, and they are tied up, but that's not the answer," Clare said. "They will turn soon. All of them."

Mason sighed. "I know."

"How many are there?" Clare asked.

"Twenty-two, including three children," Blanca said.

"Oh, my God. Kids?" Clare echoed.

"Sedate them. That way, they won't feel anything," Madeleine, the head matron, suggested.

"We don't have enough sedatives," Ruby replied.

"Do we have enough for the children, at least?" Madeleine asked.

"Yes, we do," Ruby confirmed.

"Alright. I'll sedate them, and their parents can sit with them until the end," Madeleine said. "When the time comes, I can end it quickly and painlessly."

"I'll help you," Ruby said.

"Thank you," Madeleine said, looking relieved.

"Blanca, can you post a guard to each of them too?" Mason asked. "When it comes to kids, the parents might do desperate things."

"Alright. I'll see to it," Blanca said.

"What about the adults?" Mason asked, addressing the elephant in the room.

"Give them a choice. That's what I would want," Clare said. "Take your chances out there, or end it here."

"It is the best option," Priya said, looking at her team. "We can take care of it. This is our responsibility. Our people."

"Are you sure?" Mason asked.

"Yes," Priya said.

"Alright, that's decided. Is there anything else?" Mason asked. When no one volunteered anything, he added, "Then I suggest we complete our tasks for the night and get some sleep. We will need it."

One by one, the crowd dispersed until only Clare and Mason remained. Mason shifted from one foot to the other, feeling awkward and uncertain. "I'm going to miss you, Sis."

"I'll miss you too, Bro. Be careful out there," Clare said.

"I'll try," Mason said with a nod.

"Come here and give me a hug," Clare said, waving him in.

Hugging his sister for what might be the last time, Mason wondered if he was doing the right thing, continuing the war. An eye for an eye. That was what Amelia and a few of the others wanted. All he wanted was the chance to live in peace. "Am I doing the right thing, Sis?"

"Yes, you are. Someone needs to keep Amelia and the others

in line. If you don't, they'll become monsters, too," Clare said. "Be the voice of reason."

"I don't know if I can do this. If I can go out and kill people in cold blood, no matter what they did to us," Mason admitted.

"Don't think of it like that. Think of it as defending your family. We'll never be able to live in peace as long as they are out there," Clare said.

"Alright. I'll do my best," Mason said.

"I expect nothing less," Clare replied.

Chapter 21 - Priya

Priya left the meeting with a heavy heart. Although she had volunteered for the task, she was not looking forward to it. From the expressions on their faces, neither did Chris or Matt, though they understood the necessity, as did she.

Blanca didn't seem to care, though it was hard to tell from her cold expression. Sometimes, she came across as heartless, yet at other times, she displayed a surprising amount of feeling. This was not one of those times.

"Are you guys okay with doing this?" Priya asked, giving them the option to back out.

"No, but I'm doing it anyway," Matt said. "That way, no one else has to do it."

Typical Matt. Always thinking of others, Priya thought.

"We don't have a choice," Chris said.

"I know, but you can sit this one out," Priya said.

"And abandon my team? No way," Chris said, loyal to the end.

"What about you, Blanca?" Priya asked.

"It has to be done," Blanca said. "The sooner, the better. Less suffering."

Priya could not argue with that. In the final stages, the disease caused a lot of pain, and no one wanted to see others suffer like that. Sometimes, they died quickly, and sometimes, it took hours. Even days.

There was the fever, the bleeding, the fading in and out of consciousness, delirium, skin rashes, vomiting, cramps… and excruciating pain. *Rather end it before it gets to that point.*

It reminded her of her own injuries, and she scratched at the stitches on her palms. Some of the cuts had been too deep for a simple bandage, and Madeleine had stitched them up, mainly on her palms, forearms, and legs. The rest were disinfected and bandaged, and she was given a course of antibiotics to prevent infection. Still, banged up as she was, she was still alive. *Unlike these poor people. They're dead men walking.*

Once they reached the quarantine room, Priya dispatched three guards along with the infected children to separate rooms where Madeleine and Ruby waited to sedate them. It was sad to see the little ones go, knowing they wouldn't live to see another day, but at least they wouldn't feel anything.

Their families were a different story, however, and Priya's heart went out to the grieving parents. They stumbled out of the room, shoulders bowed, shocked, and disbelieving. Some were angry, others sobbed. But no matter how they reacted, their pain was real and visceral.

Once they were gone, Priya turned her attention to the remaining adults and cleared her throat. "As you know, you have all been infected with the disease, and within the next few hours, you'll turn."

"How do you know this for sure?" one guy protested. "We only have your word for it."

"Ours and the millions of zombies out there," Priya pointed out.

"That still doesn't mean we'll turn," he replied. "What if we're

CHAPTER 21 - PRIYA

immune?"

"That's a chance we can't take," Priya said. "You are a danger to all of us, and so far, no reports or signs of immunity to the disease have surfaced."

"So, you're just going to kill us all?" the man asked, his face turning pale. "That's murder!"

"No, we are not killing you," Priya said.

"What then?"

"We're giving you a choice. You can leave and take your chances out there, or you can end it yourselves. One bullet for a quick and painless death," Priya said.

"That's not a choice at all," the man protested.

"If you send us out, we'll die," another added.

"The zombies will kill us," a woman cried.

"If you stay, you could kill us all," Priya pointed out. "We do not have the facilities or personnel to wait until you turn before we put you down. It could happen at any moment, and thirty-plus fresh zombies will cause havoc in here."

"She's right," another man spoke up. "You know she's right. This place doesn't have neat little cells where they can lock us up or a bunch of soldiers who can watch us around the clock. One mistake and this whole place goes down."

"Yeah, right," the first man to protest said, snorting. "They could tie us up or something."

"Have you seen how strong a fresh zombie is?" the other man replied. "I've got a wife and child here. I won't endanger them. I'll take the bullet."

Priya closed her eyes and swallowed, secretly horrified. "Thank you, Sir."

"Well, I'm not taking the bullet. I want out," the other man said.

"That's your choice," Priya said. "Those who want to leave, stand over there."

For a long moment, no one moved except for the protester. Then the dam broke, and the rest followed. All but the first man to volunteer for the bullet, and two more. A woman and a teenage boy.

Priya eyed the people who wanted to leave and asked, "Are you sure? Once you leave, you can't come back. You can't hang around either. If we spot you lurking around outside the fence, we'll shoot."

One by one, they nodded.

"Alright. Chris, Matt, please escort them to the gates and make certain they leave the area," Priya said. "But give them a few minutes to say goodbye to any friends and family."

"Yes, ma'am," Chris and Matt said, herding the infected outside with the help of six extra guards.

Priya watched them leave with mixed emotions. Though she would've taken the bullet herself, she understood their reasons. No one wanted to die, and they would rather take a chance at being immune or even becoming a zombie. Anything was better than death for those who weren't ready to die.

That left the other three, and she turned to them with reluctance. "Are you ready?"

"Yes, ma'am," the man replied with a decisive nod.

The woman shook like a leaf, but she nodded too. "I'm ready."

The teenage boy bit his lip. "Can you do it for me?"

Priya sucked in a deep breath, and her entire being rebelled against the thought. But the sight of the boy's tears was enough to sway her, and she nodded. "Okay."

"Thank you," he whispered.

"Alright," Priya said, stepping aside. "You can say your

CHAPTER 21 - PRIYA

goodbyes, and then we'll go outside."

A number of people streamed into the room, and a tearful farewell ensued, the kind that tugged at Priya's heartstrings. She turned her back and dashed away the tears, not wanting to see the grief in the families' eyes. It was too much.

Finally, it was over. Priya waved at three guards to accompany her, Blanca, and the three infected out of the building. Outside, they found a secluded spot hidden from prying eyes and windows.

Swallowing hard on the knot in her throat, Priya looked at the teenage boy. "Would you like to go first?"

The boy nodded. "Will it hurt?"

"No, it won't. I promise," Priya said, tears pricking her eyelids.

"O... okay."

Leading him around a corner, she said, "Turn away. Don't look."

The boy obeyed, and she added. "Think of something nice. Like your best memory. Don't think about me or the gun."

"Alright," the boy said, shivering in the chill wind.

Raising her gun, Priya nerved herself to shoot. Her hand wobbled, and she sucked in a deep breath. *Don't screw this up, damn it. Quick and painless.*

Her hand steadied. She owed the boy a clean death.

Bang!

The boy collapsed, his legs folding up underneath him. He tipped over, and blood leaked from the hole in his skull. The bullet had done its job, and his death was both painless and instant. For him, the nightmare was over, but not for Priya.

She staggered and almost went down, her vision turning black around the edges, but she somehow managed to steady herself. While she might feel like a murderer, she still had a job to finish. Besides Blanca, the other three guards were watching. She couldn't afford to lose her shit in front of them.

Straightening up, she took a deep breath and went back. The woman went next, putting the barrel in her mouth. Finally, the man, his hands steady and his expression one of peace.

Once it was over, Priya waited until the bodies were buried in shallow graves for the family to visit. She mumbled a quick prayer, holding onto her composure long enough to make it to the nearest bathroom.

There, she retched into the nearest toilet, slamming the door shut behind her. She heaved until her stomach was empty, and spots danced in front of her eyes. It was cathartic but also pointless. The hurt remained, an iron fist squeezing her heart whenever she remembered the boy's haunted eyes.

Afterward, Priya splashed cold water on her face and stared at her expression in the mirror. A stranger looked back at her, and she knew she'd never be the same again. For the boy, the bullet that pierced his brain meant the end of his suffering. For her, it was just the beginning.

Chapter 22 - George

The next morning, George woke up bright and early. Now that the time had come to leave, he couldn't wait and wanted to get moving. Saying goodbye to his friends and fellow firefighters was hard, though, and he approached the task with a heavy heart. Still, he had to move on and start a new chapter in his life. With only one arm, he'd never be the fighter he used to be, and the role of trader slash farmer appealed to him.

He shook hands with Mason, Elijah, Benjamin, Mike, Leo, Frank, and Rick, and said goodbye to all the ladies: Clare, Susan, Ruby, Ellen, and Theresa.

"Thank you for everything, Theresa. I'll miss you," George said, hugging the older woman.

"I'll miss you too, George. Be sure to visit often," Theresa replied.

"Of course. I'll see all of you very soon. I promise," George replied.

And he was confident he'd get to see them again. The whole point of his leaving was to establish a trade route between the farmers and the island. A daunting task but one he looked forward to. Besides, he'd have help in the form of Timothy, who knew the entire farming community.

Finally, he came face to face with Amelia, and his words

dried up like droplets of water in the desert sun. This was the moment he'd avoided for as long as possible. The moment he'd have to say farewell to his quarantine buddy and good friend. "Amelia."

Amelia stared back at him, her expression stern. "George."

"I, uh… I'm going to miss you," he stuttered.

"I should hope so," she replied, still not giving a hint as to her feelings.

"I'm sorry, I'm not staying, but I can't. Not now," he said.

"I know."

Sticking out his hand, he said, "Goodbye, Amelia."

Blinking furiously, Amelia said, "Come here, you stupid lug. Give me a hug."

Relief flowed through his veins, and he grinned as he pulled her close. "I thought you were mad at me."

"I am mad at you, but I'll get over it," Amelia said, brushing away tears. "Look after yourself, and stay out of trouble."

"I will," George said, stepping back. With a knot in his throat, he waved at the assembled firefighters. "Bye, everyone. I hope to see you all again one day."

Throwing his backpack into the Jeep, George prepared to leave. He placed Sebastian's carrier on the backseat and climbed behind the wheel. "Don't worry, Sebastian. Soon, you'll have an entire farm at your disposal. You'll be free to roam wherever you want, zombie-free."

Sebastian didn't bother to answer, too engrossed in grooming his paws and nibbling on a treat of dried meat.

Minutes later, George was joined by Timothy, and he asked, "Ready to go?"

"Almost," Timothy replied.

"What's the hold-up?"

CHAPTER 22 - GEORGE

"We're waiting for more people."

"More people?" George said, confused. "I thought it was just us."

"It would've been except for a couple of last-minute changes," Timothy replied with a grin.

Suddenly, the Jeep's back doors opened, and two figures jumped in, each carrying an oversized backpack. It was Priya and Sarah, the last people he'd ever have expected to join the farm expedition. "What are you two doing here?"

Sarah made herself comfortable beside Sebastian and said, 'We can't let you have all the fun!"

"Fun? What fun?" George asked.

"Exactly. Without us, this mission is doomed to misery and failure," Sarah added, as irrepressible as always.

"I just need a change of scenery," Priya said, her expression smooth.

"A change of scenery? This is more than just a change," George repeated, shaking his head. "Are you sure about doing this?"

"I have never been surer of anything in my life," Priya said, their gaze meeting in the rearview mirror. Cuts and bruises marred her skin, but he didn't notice. What he noticed was the look in her eyes.

Within them, George glimpsed a hidden well of loss and grief, and suddenly her decision made sense. She wanted what he did: A new beginning away from everything and everyone they'd lost.

In that regard, they were kindred souls. In every other regard, however, they were polar opposites, and George didn't know how he felt about having her along. She definitely complicated matters, and he wondered how they'd co-exist. *I guess only time will tell.*

Chapter 23 - Clare

After George left, taking Timothy, Priya, and Sarah with him, Clare returned to the task at hand: Relocating everyone to the second safe house. It was far better equipped, fortified, and supplied than the one they were at, and she couldn't wait to leave. "We don't even have any coffee."

"I know," Mason said, looking bleary-eyed.

"Yup, soup is all you're gonna get. Canned potato and leek, watered down with broth," Susan said, handing each of them a bowl.

"Ugh, no thanks," Clare said, wrinkling her nose.

"Just eat it," Susan said. "You're setting a bad example."

Looking around, Clare was ashamed to see the many faces staring at her, their new leader, and she was complaining about crap. They'd lost not only their home but loved ones the night before. "I'm sorry. I guess I need to be more aware of my actions from now on."

"Exactly," Susan said. "Lead by example."

Taking the soup, Clare ate every drop, careful not to pull a face at the chalky taste. Afterward, she planned out the last details of their move with Mason. "You're staying here for now, right?"

"Only until we can find a better place to stay," Mason said.

"This place is too big for just a handful of us to defend. Besides, there's no coffee."

Clare chuckled. "I hear you."

"For you, it's a straight shot from here to the second safe house," Mason said, indicating the route on a map. "It's right on the docks, and you should be able to find boats to take you across to the island."

"First, we'll scout the area and check it out. It might not be habitable or safe," Clare said.

"Probably not. That's where the hard work comes in, but I know you can do it. There's plenty of material you can scavenge along the docks, and it's away from the city center."

"That's the plan," Clare said, bobbing her head. "Scout the island, clear it of infected, make it secure, set up a camp, and build a new home for us all."

"See?" Mason said with a grin. "Easy peasy!"

"We can leave you a vehicle or two with fuel and a couple of the guns. Plus, there's plenty of soup," Clare offered.

"You can keep the soup, but I'll take the guns, no problem." Mason sighed. "How to win a war? Any tips, Sis?"

"Sure. Scout the area, find the bad men, kill them, leave them to rot, and come home. Easy peasy," Clare said with a grin.

"Ugh, you are the worst," Mason said with a groan. "But I suppose that just about covers it. Anything else?"

"Can you get the vehicles ready, please? And make sure everything is loaded up and ready to go. Including the soup," Clare asked.

"No problem," Mason said, standing up. "What about you?"

"I think it's time I talked to my new charges. They need to know what they're in for," she replied.

"Good luck," Mason said, leaving her to it.

CHAPTER 23 - CLARE

Climbing up on a chair, Clare called out. "Hello? Can I have everyone's attention, please?"

The room stilled, and every face turned toward her. Young and old, they all looked to her for answers, and she prayed she could find the words they needed to hear.

"I know you are scared and tired; I know you've lost people. Family and friends. I've lost people too. I'm scared too. But I promise you. I will do my best to ensure your safety, health, and prosperity, now and in the future," Clare said.

A murmur rang through the crowd, followed by questions, each more urgent than the last. The people needed reassurance, whether real or fake, it didn't matter.

"Where are we going?"

"What are we supposed to do?"

"We've got no food. No home."

"What about the zombies?"

"Are we going to die?"

Holding her hand up, Clare waited until silence settled across the room once more. "Do not worry. We have a plan. Within the next hour or two, we are leaving for a second safe house. This one is well-fortified and supplied. We can stay there for a few weeks while we plan our next move."

"What's the next move?" one man called out.

"Building a settlement on Burlington Island," Clare replied.

Disbelief rippled through the crowd before she was bombarded with the inevitable doubts and questions from dozens of frightened minds.

"There's nothing out there."

"Where will we stay?"

"What will we eat?"

"What about the infected?"

"It's too exposed."

Clare raised her hands again, patiently waiting for the hubbub to die down once more. When the room fell quiet, she answered as many of the questions as possible.

"We'll build new homes, plant crops, fish in the river, and set up defenses. We will do it because we have to. Because no one else is going to do it for us. We will do it because if we don't, the only thing that awaits us is starvation and death. We will do it because we have no other choice."

Looking around the room, she noted each one of her people. Her community. The individuals she had sworn to protect. The lives Kingsley had sacrificed himself for. That so many had died for.

"This is where we make our stand. This is where we decide if we want to live or die. But I cannot make that choice for you. Only you can."

"How? What do we do?" a woman asked.

"Make your own decision. If that decision includes fighting for your lives and working your fingers to the bone for a new future, you are welcome to join me at the second safe house. If not, you are free to make your own way out there in the city, and I wish you good luck. You have thirty minutes to decide. If you are not on one of the vehicles from the convoy after that, you're on your own."

Jumping down from the chair, Clare made her way outside. Mason saw her coming and whistled. "That was some tough love."

"I thought they deserved to know what was waiting for them in the days ahead and to make up their own minds," Clare said. "It won't be easy, and people should know what they're in for."

"Fair enough," Mason said. "Now, let's see how many take

CHAPTER 23 - CLARE

you up on your offer."

"I think they might surprise us," Clare said. "Besides, where else would they go? Fear is a great motivator."

Clare's words proved to be prophetic. Thirty minutes later, every person inside the safe house was loaded onto a vehicle and ready to go. Not a single soul had opted out. The only ones hanging back were Mason and his small group of fighters.

"Huh, I guess your little speech worked," Mason said.

"I can see that," Clare replied, more than a little surprised despite her earlier confidence.

"Well. I guess this is it," Mason said. "This is goodbye."

"For now," Clare acknowledged. "Keep an eye on that radio, will you? I'll be in touch. George too."

"I will. Never fear," Mason replied.

Behind her, the convoy was loaded and ready to go. The whole community waited for her, but still, she hesitated.

"What are you waiting for?" Mason asked. "Your people need you. Go."

"Can I get another hug, Bro?" Clare asked.

"What? The second one in as many days?" Mason exclaimed. "This is becoming ridiculous." Still laughing, he scooped her into his arms and hugged her close. "Is that better?"

"Much better," Clare said, breathing in his familiar scent. It calmed her nerves and settled her stomach. No matter what happened, he would always be her older brother, and they'd always have each others' backs.

Chapter 24 - Zoey

Zoey stayed awake the entire night, waiting for Banks' signal. It was impossible to sleep while surrounded by Blackwell and his men anyway. After his initial temper tantrum, the leader soon waxed lyrical about his latest triumph, and an all-out celebration ensued.

Hidden in her dark corner, Zoey tried to keep out of it and succeeded for the most part. Whenever it looked like someone might approach her, Banks ran interference. He distracted them with booze, jokes, and anything else that might redirect their attention.

That tactic did not work on either Lucien or Blackwell. Both sauntered over at one point, intent on torturing her with their evil presence.

"You should be grateful," Lucien said, favoring her with a sneer.

"Oh? How so?" Zoey asked, raising her chin.

"Not many have been given the chance to join Blackwell's group. You're one of the few, and you should be more appreciative. In fact," Lucien said, flashing Blackwell an amused look, "you should be groveling at his feet."

"Mm, I like that idea," Blackwell said, his eyes gleaming. "Groveling sounds like fun."

CHAPTER 24 - ZOEY

"Grovel? After you shot and tortured me?" Zoe asked, aghast.

"Shooting you was an accident," Lucien said. "How many times do I have to say it?"

"The torturing was not an accident," Zoey said.

"We needed information," Lucien pointed out. "It worked, didn't it?"

"I don't know. Did it?" Zoey asked, intent on pissing him off. "Last I heard, half of the hospital community escaped your murderous efforts and blew up half of the supplies."

"An exaggeration," Lucien said. "Everything will be fine in the morning."

"Why? What's so special about the morning?" Zoey asked, needling him some more.

"In the morning, we'll clear away the infected, and the hospital will be ours," Lucien said.

"Will it? Or are you just fooling yourself?" Zoey said. "I mean, you already fucked up once."

"Ooh, she's got you there," Blackwell crowed.

"Just shut up, will you? Both of you!" Lucien snapped before he stormed away.

Blackwell eyed her, clearly amused. "You shouldn't anger him. That man has no conscience and zero remorse. He doesn't think the way you do."

"Neither do you," Zoey said.

"Oh, I feel remorse. Just not for the same things you do. Plus, I'm a little crazy," Blackwell said with a crooked smile.

Zoey pondered that as he walked away, wondering what he meant, but gave up after a while.

Banks moved closer. "What did they want?"

"To irritate me, what else?" Zoey said. "Just like you're doing now."

Banks sighed. "Be ready. It'll be soon."

"Whatever," Zoey muttered, not in the mood to talk.

"And again, I'm sorry, Zoey. I didn't want any of this to happen," Banks said.

"Well, you got it whether you wanted it or not," Zoey said in a fierce whisper. "Our friends are gone. Dead. And we're stuck here, celebrating that fact with their murderers."

Banks nodded but didn't reply. Instead, he got up and walked away, loitering in the far corners of the room. Zoey stopped paying attention after a while but perked up when a fight broke out between two of the men.

They went at it with their fists, and she noticed Banks edging closer to the struggling duo. Suddenly, he lunged forward and yanked the gun from one of their belts. Backing up, he aimed the weapon at the room in general. At the same time, he waved Zoey toward the exit. "Run, Zoey! Run!"

Zoey jumped to her feet but froze when Blackwell spoke. "Don't listen to him. You know you won't get very far. It's dark outside, the streets are full of zombies, and you've got nowhere to go."

"Run, damn it," Banks yelled, urging her on.

"Don't be stupid," Blackwell said with a taunting smile. "If you stay, I'll make sure you get treated right."

"He's lying. You know that, Zoey," Banks said.

Looking from one to the other, Zoey tried to make up her mind, but it was hard to think straight with so much fear coursing through her veins. On the one hand, she was deathly afraid of the outside world. She'd only ever seen it from inside the ambulance. On the other, she wanted nothing more than to get away from Blackwell and his men.

"With me, you'll be safe, warm, and protected," Blackwell

said, easing toward her. He raised his hands, trying to calm her like a spooked horse.

"Stop right there. Don't move," Banks cried.

Blackwell ignored him and kept moving, slowly but surely.

"Banks? What do I do?" Zoey cried, desperate for guidance.

Their eyes met across the distance, and Banks said, "I got you into this, Zoey. I messed up. Let me make it right."

"O...okay," Zoey replied, dashing for the exit. Blackwell followed, and Banks shot at him. One, two, three times.

The third shot hit Blackwell in the leg, and he went down hard. Immediately, all hell broke loose. Lucien launched himself at Banks while the rest ran toward Blackwell.

Zoey sprinted across the open space until she hit the door. Yanking it open, she looked back. Banks was down with Lucien on top of him, and Blackwell bellowed with murderous rage. "Bring him to me, the son of a bitch. I'll kill him with my bare hands. And someone go after the woman. Bring her back alive!"

With those words ringing in her ears, Zoey sprinted into the cold wintry night, unarmed and utterly lost. She had no idea where she was or where she was going. The only thing she knew was that she had to escape.

Behind her, a single shot rang out, and she faltered. *Please, no. Don't let it be him. Don't let it be Banks. No matter what he did, I still love him.*

But the night had no answers for her, and Zoey forced herself to keep going. If Banks was dead, she needed to honor his sacrifice, which meant gaining her freedom from the tyranny of Blackwell and his men. No matter what it cost.

Epilogue I - Clare

Clare lifted the pickax, swung it overhead, and brought it down in one smooth motion. The pointed metal end sank deep into the ground, breaking up the hard soil and loosening the rocks. She repeated the maneuver over and over again, forming a smooth rhythm. With each swing, the muscles in her back, shoulders, and arms stretched and contracted with the effort. Sweat pooled underneath her armpits and dripped from her chin.

It was backbreaking labor, but she didn't mind. It kept her thoughts away from her brother and his team in Burlington and free from worry for their safety. She couldn't afford to lose focus. Not when she had an entire community to look after and keep safe from harm.

Thankfully, the second safe house had proved to be exactly what they needed to lick their wounds, shore up their flagging morale, and build their strength. The wounded and the ill recovered, the children bounced back, and everyone got to grieve in peace for lost loved ones.

During that time, Clare and her friends commandeered a small fleet of boats, scouted the island, cleared it of infection, and fixed up a few of the small buildings. They also built barricades blocking off the promenade, Burlington Bristol bridge, and the deer crossover on the northern side. A strong fence around the living area finished off the basic preparations, and they were ready to move everyone over.

That was two weeks ago. Since then, they'd quickly settled in. Dirk and a team of volunteers were busy installing solar systems, getting the plumbing up and running, and digging a couple of boreholes. Generators provided electricity for a few hours a day, and raiding teams gathered more supplies from the surrounding city and docks.

Ruby operated the clinic with the help of Madeleine Koch, and together they cared for the community's medical needs. Susan and Lindsey ran the field kitchen, feeding the masses, while Theresa coordinated the work teams, drew up the daily rosters, and sorted out the rations. A handful of parents and teachers minded the children and kept up with their schooling while a team of guards under Blanca's command patrolled the fences and took out any infected.

It wasn't easy overseeing so many different people, especially the survivors from the hospital community. After riding out the worst of the apocalypse in relative comfort, they weren't used to fending for themselves. Frank had his hands full teaching them how to defend themselves, and they balked at heavy labor.

Luckily, Clare had the support of the remaining hospital board: Madeleine, Lindsey, and Dirk. She also had Blanca in her corner, thanks to Priya, and soon, Mason and the rest would return. Hopefully, with Blackwell's head on a platter.

With a sigh, Clare pushed the thought aside. As fun as it was to dream about Blackwell's death, there was work to be done. Once she finished digging up her demarcated plot, she picked out any rocks, brush, and weeds and loaded them onto a wheelbarrow for dumping.

Elijah and Benjamin moved in next, creating neat rows ready for planting winter crops, a mixture of potatoes, onions, carrots, squash, leeks, and cabbage. They hoped to have a harvest within a few months. The first of many.

"Looking good," Susan said, walking over with a cooler bag filled with bottled water. "Anyone thirsty?"

"Thanks. I'm dying over here," Clare said, gratefully accepting a bottle. She twisted open the top and took a couple of deep swigs. The cool liquid felt like heaven to her parched tissues, and she let out a groan of appreciation.

"Things are looking up," Susan said, looking around. "We've come a long way."

"That we have," Clare agreed, surveying their handiwork. "It's nowhere near what we had before, but it's better than nothing."

"We'll get there," Elijah said, walking over.

"At least we have a roof over our heads, and we're safe from zombies," Benjamin agreed.

"Have you seen what the kids are doing?" Susan asked.

"Nope. What is it?" Clare asked.

"They're building a remembrance wall."

"Really?" Clare asked, touched despite herself.

"Yup. Brick by brick, they're building a wall and painting each one with someone's name. It's beautiful."

"Wow. Remind me to swing by after work," Clare said. "I can say hello to Paisley too."

"Mm, good idea," Susan said. "Sometimes, I think you work too hard."

"Leading by example and all that," Clare said with a shrug.

"And doing a great job of it," Elijah said.

EPILOGUE I - CLARE

"I wonder how Mason and the others are doing," Susan said, handing out more water.

"Last I heard, they were watching Blackwell and his crew. Those assholes have settled into the hospital, living high on the hog," Clare said. "There's still no sign of either Banks or Zoey."

"Bastards," Elijah muttered, his expression darkening. "I should be with Mason, helping him kill those assholes. Not sitting here playing farmhand."

"They'll get what's coming to them. Mason will make sure of that," Susan said.

"But I won't be there to see it," Elijah said.

"I know how you feel. I want to be there too, but Ruby needs you," Clare said. "this place needs us, and what we're doing here is just as important as chasing bad guys."

"I guess," Elijah muttered, not entirely convinced.

"Just look around," Clare said, waving a hand around. "When we got here, there was nothing. Now, look at it. We have the beginnings of a community here. A future for us and our children."

"She's right," Susan said. "We've got food in our bellies, a roof over our heads, and kids playing in the sunlight. This is our new home."

"We lost our homes," Elijah said, looking glum. "Twice.

"No, we didn't," Clare said, reaching out to squeeze his hand. "We are our home. Home is not a place. It's us."

"It's a nice idea," Elijah admitted.

"And in time, it will become a reality," Clare said.

"Well, if anyone can get it done, it's you," Elijah said.

"Thanks." Gazing around, Clare vowed not to give up. Not to stop until they and everyone who sought refuge with them were safe, happy, and healthy. *This is it. This is where we'll make history.*

Epilogue II - Mason

Mason walked around the perimeter of his new home with slow steps, his boots crunching across the gravel. The sun hung low on the horizon, the sky streaked orange and purple. The deepening shadows loomed across the docks, and the smell of the Delaware River hung rich in the air.

Behind him squatted the warehouse they'd commandeered, a rusted square of corrugated iron, crumbling bricks, and peeling paint. Its windows were small and high in the walls, grimy with dirt. They were useless for general visibility but made for an excellent sniper's nest, and his team took turns keeping watch from its lofty heights.

He turned a corner, pausing to look around. Nothing stirred in the gathering gloom. Neither the living nor the dead. They'd covered their tracks well, and he was grateful for the rules he'd laid down initially.

Number one, no unnecessary movement, noise, or lights. Number two, guards on duty around the clock. Three, take care of the undead swiftly, silently, and hide the bodies afterward. Four, ensure you're not being followed, take a roundabout route, and stay alert. Five, no chatter on the radio, and only use secure lines.

The rules were simple and designed to protect them from

zombies and Blackwell's men. So far, it had worked, and he was confident their hiding spot was still undiscovered. They just had to keep it that way.

Satisfied that the area was clear, the fence intact, and the gates locked, he went in for the night. As Mason stepped inside, a blast of warm air enveloped him. Grateful for the heat, he rubbed his arms and stamped his feet, restoring his blood circulation.

Ellen spotted him and waved him over to their tiny kitchen, a makeshift affair cobbled together by stuff they'd gathered. A gas stove, cupboards filled with the essentials, a table topped with chopping blocks, knives, pots and pans, a camping washbasin, and a couple of buckets.

"You're just in time for a pot of freshly brewed coffee," she said, her soft blonde hair gleaming in the low light of the lanterns. She poured a cup and handed it over.

"Thanks," he said with a smile.

Overhasty, he took a sip, and the hot brew burned his throat. "Ow!"

"Careful," Ellen said with a grin. "Like I said. Freshly brewed."

Mason grimaced. "Noted."

He sought out a nearby chair and sat down, easing his long legs out in front of him. He was bone tired and longed to go to bed, but it was too early. If he went to bed now, he'd be up in a couple of hours, wide awake and unable to sleep. Instead, he looked around, studying their temporary home.

The interior consisted of a single large storage room at the front. This had become their war room, and a large table took up the center. More tables and chairs filled the space, along with crates of supplies, weapons, and anything else they'd been able to scavenge. Cleaning supplies leaned against the far wall, a reminder that it was his turn to mop the floors in the morning.

At the back, they'd discovered a few offices and a bathroom, which they converted into rough living quarters. Although the building was cold and drafty, they'd stopped up the gaps with cloth, bolted down loose sheets of iron, and covered the windows with newspapers. Old carpets covered the floors, and a gas heater chased away the wintry chill. It wasn't perfect, and tempers often frayed with the lack of space, but it was comfortable enough.

Besides Ellen and himself, it was quiet inside the warehouse. Rick helped Ellen with dinner while Matt kept watch in the sniper's nest up top. Amelia and Daisy were on a scouting mission, while Leo, Mike, and Matt were on a scavenging hunt. They needed more guns and ammunition before hoping to take on the enemy.

Thoughts of Blackwell caused Mason to frown. The man had cost them everything. Their home, their supplies, their safety, and many, many innocent lives. All because of his greed and arrogance. *He won't get away with it. I'll make sure of that.*

With a grunt, Mason shoved the thoughts aside. It would only sour his mood, and he needed to stay positive. At least Clare and the others were faring well on the island. They'd reclaimed the space from nature and the undead and turned it into a growing community.

It didn't surprise him. He'd always known his sister was capable of great things. She only needed to realize it for herself. *You're stronger than you know, Clare. Much, much stronger.*

Leaning back in his chair, his eyes began to droop. Finally, he realized he'd lost the fight and stood up. Good night, everyone.

"I think I'll turn in."

"Are you sure?" Ellen asked, waving a ladle at a bubbling pot on the stove. "The food's almost ready."

"I can't keep my eyes open," Mason admitted.

"All right. I'll save you a plate," she replied, patting him on the back.

He nodded and headed towards his sleeping quarters, a small corner in one of the offices. A camping cot and a thin mattress on the floor awaited. It wasn't much, but it was better than nothing.

As he drifted off to sleep, Mason couldn't shake the feeling they had to hurry. Blackwell was no fool, and it was only a matter of time before their hiding spot was discovered. They had to strike Blackwell, but to do that, they needed intel. *Amelia, Daisy. Wherever you are, we need that information. We're all counting on you now.*

Epilogue III - George

George woke up well before dawn. Life on a farm started long before the sun was up. That much he'd learned early on. John, Timothy's father, was fair, but he brooked no nonsense and expected everyone to pull their weight. They all had jobs, from the youngest to the oldest. Even the visitors.

The day after they arrived, George and Timothy moved into the bunkhouse at the back of the farmhouse, sharing the space with four others. They were all young men, single, with nowhere else to go. John offered them food, shelter, and safety during the apocalypse in return for their labor on the farm. It was a good deal, and George was happy to fall into the routine.

Solidly built, the bunkhouse was well insulated against the elements. One half consisted of a row of bunk beds, and the other half made up a small lounge and kitchen. On cold nights, a wood-burning stove kept the rooms warm and cozy while a pot of coffee simmered on the coals. A shelf lined with books and a couple of board games provided entertainment, while the solid oak doors and barred windows ensured their safety.

Priya and Sarah stayed in the farmhouse since John did not deem it appropriate for unmarried men and women to share sleeping quarters. Old school, he preferred keeping the sexes separate.

While it was much more luxurious than the bunkhouse, George didn't mind. They all worked equally hard to keep the place running, feeding the animals, tending to the crops, maintaining the infrastructure, checking the fences, and patrolling the roads.

They were almost ready to make their first run to the island, as well. The route had been thoroughly scouted and cleared. Supply caches were set up strategically, with three vehicles fueled and ready to go.

At night, everyone gathered around a fire, drank a beer or two, and talked nonsense until bedtime. It was a simple life, but George liked it. Out on the land, the stresses of modern-day life did not exist. There was no rat race, no crime, and hardly any zombies. If he closed his eyes, he could almost pretend the apocalypse had never happened.

Almost.

He still had nightmares about Bobbi. In his dreams, he relived her awful death. He felt the slick warmth of her blood coating his hands and the gun bucking in his hand. The sound of that fatal shot haunted him, as did her vacant eyes, empty of all expression.

Sebastian missed her too. While he'd adapted to life on the farm with remarkable ease, he sometimes sought George out on a cold, wintry night, looking for comfort. They'd sit together in silence, gazing into the flickering flames of the fire while they remembered what they'd lost.

But Bobbi wouldn't have wanted either of them to mourn forever. She was far too practical for that. She'd want them to live their lives to the fullest, even Sebastian, who lived for catching rats and lazing in the sun nowadays.

With that thought in mind, George grabbed a cup of coffee

and stepped onto the porch. Situated on a low rise, the farm spread out in all directions, a vast panorama of rolling green hills dotted with stands of spruce and pine.

The first rays of the sun touched the horizon, bathing the fields with gold. Streaks of lavender lit up the sky, and a crisp breeze swirled through the knee-high grass. It was a stirring sight, and he realized once again how lucky he was to end up in such a place.

Sure, he missed his old home and his firefighter friends. He worried about Mason and his group back in the city. They faced a dangerous venture, taking out Blackwell and his accomplices, and he wished them luck. He also hoped Clare and her group would succeed in building a home on the island, but he felt no need to join them. *I've got everything I want right here.*

The sound of a door opening drew his attention to the farmhouse, and he spotted Priya and Sarah out and about. Together, they walked toward the chicken coop to fetch eggs for breakfast, laughing and talking along the way.

They'd settled in much faster than he'd have thought possible. Being city girls, he'd expected a period filled with growing pains. Instead, they knuckled down and threw themselves into the farm life with abandon.

On the way back to the house, Priya noticed him and waved. "Come on up. Breakfast is almost ready!"

"Thanks! I'll be right there," George replied, emptying his coffee cup.

Timothy was probably already at the house, studying the route they'd mapped out for their island run. Not only did they have to get there and back in one piece, but they also had to stop at other farms along the way and pick up more supplies.

It was a complicated venture, but George looked forward to it, just like he looked forward to spending the rest of his life out in the country. Here, far away from everything and everyone he'd known, he finally felt at peace. *I'm home, Bobbi. I'm finally home.*

Epilogue IV- Nikki

After her near-disastrous encounter with the family in the blue sedan, Nikki vowed not to let anything else get in her way. She also wasn't going to keep her promise of trying to find more fuel for the family. That ship had sailed the minute the father opened fire on her, guaranteeing his doom. The thought of an entire family succumbing to the apocalypse was a gloomy one, but she tried not to dwell on it.

Shaking her head, she said, "He should've taken the lift."

Cooper whined in agreement, still tense after the encounter. It'd taken a long time for him to calm down, and she had to give him lots of extra cuddles to make up for it. Now, she vowed to put the ordeal behind her. It was over, and they were still alive. Wiser, too. "You can't trust anyone in this world. Especially someone who has a lot to lose."

Looking at the map, she noticed that Burlington was only half a day's drive away. With any luck, they could make it before sunset. That left them enough time to find a suitable shelter for the night, preferably one with running water and a working toilet. A bath or shower would be even better, but she didn't want to get her hopes up.

The thought of reaching the end of her journey buoyed her flagging morale, and she looked forward to her arrival. While she wasn't dumb enough to think that finding George would be easy, it did bring her one step closer.

"What do you say, Cooper? Are you as excited as I am?" Nikki asked, ruffling the dog's fur. "We're nearly there!"

"Woof!" Cooper replied before sticking his nose out of the window again. It was open just a crack, not enough for a zombie to get its hands inside, but enough for Cooper to get some fresh air.

Nikki could only imagine what he smelled and what information he gleaned from the countryside. For a moment, she almost wished she had such keen senses, but changed her mind when she remembered how much the undead stank. The thought of smelling them in vivid detail was enough to turn her stomach, and she gagged. "Yuck. No thanks. You can keep your nose to yourself, Cooper."

The dog shot her a quizzical glance, clearly thinking she was crazy. Nikki laughed and turned back to the road, confident that their journey would be much smoother in the future. The sky was clear, the road empty, the back of the truck loaded with supplies, and the tank nearly full.

"Wait, what's going on?" Nikki asked, frowning at the fuel gauge. Before her eyes, it dropped a notch, steadily decreasing with every mile that passed. Within minutes, the needle hovered below half, and panic bubbled up inside her chest. "Something's wrong. Very, very wrong."

Nikki pulled over and killed the engine as soon as she had the chance. She got out and walked around the truck with her gun in hand. When nothing grabbed her attention, she dropped to her haunches and examined the ground underneath the vehicle. A damp patch in the sand caught her eyes, and the acrid smell of fuel burned her nostrils. Leaning in, she saw a steady stream of gas leaking from the tank. "Ah, crap. How the hell did that happen?"

Still cursing, she straightened up and examined the vehicle again, looking closer this time. When she spotted it, she cursed herself for not seeing it sooner. A bullet hole in the fuel tank. "What the... Ah, this is just awesome. Freaking awesome!"

The perfectly round puncture mocked her, and Nikki wanted to scream with rage. Stomping her feet in a full-blown tantrum, she yelled, "That stupid little man. This is all his fault. Why didn't he take the damn lift?"

Throwing her hands in the air, Nikki stomped back to the front of the truck and climbed behind the wheel. She had no choice but to continue. Without the means to fix the fuel tank, she could only try to get as close to Burlington as possible. "Maybe I'm lucky, and the shot went through the top of the tank. Maybe there's enough gas left in the bottom to get us there."

Even as Nikki spoke the words, she knew how stupid that sounded. The fuel gauge continued to drop lower and lower. She willed the needle to stay in place, but it kept sinking until it hovered just above empty. The reserve light came on, and panic welled up inside her chest. "Come on, come on."

The truck cruised for a few more miles, egged on by her fervent prayers before it sputtered, shook, and died a miserable death. Despair fell over her like a blanket, thick and suffocating, and she sat frozen in her seat for several long moments. Finally, Cooper broke the spell, licking her face and nudging her with his wet nose.

Nikki sighed and scraped together her flagging reserves. She had to face facts. The truck was dead, and there was nothing around for miles. Nothing and no one. The only person she could rely on was herself. Burlington was still a long way off, and she had to get moving if she hoped to make it on foot.

"Come on, boy. I guess we're walking from here on out," Nikki said, gathering her stuff.

Cooper barked and wagged his tail, a lot happier about the thought of walking than her.

Rolling her eyes, Nikki said, "Yeah, yeah. Aren't you just loving this to bits? Don't expect me to be happy about it, though. I'm not nearly as fit as you are."

Nikki sorted through the supplies on the back of the truck, trying to decide what to take. She already had a backpack filled with clothes, toiletries, a medical aid kit, a towel, a can opener, and a water bottle. A blanket roll was tied to the bottom, and she tucked her spare gun into a side pocket.

To this, she added more food. Packets of nuts, dried fruit, protein bars, biscuits, and a jar of peanut butter. No cans because they were too heavy. She also threw in a packet of dog food for Cooper, more water, a lighter, batteries, and an extra blanket.

On her belt, she carried the other gun, the hammer she took from Rex's garage as a hand weapon, and a flashlight. She also pulled on a warm jacket, gloves, a beanie, and a scarf to ward off the cold.

Testing the pack, she found it heavy but doable. She was as prepared as she could ever hope to be, and it was time to hit the road. "Right. That should do it."

Still, Nikki hesitated, unable to take the leap. She clung to the truck's side, loathe to leave the familiar. It felt strange to head out on foot, exposed to the elements and worse: Zombies.

Cooper whined and pressed his nose to her leg as if he felt her anxiety. She scratched him behind one ear and said, "Don't worry, boy. We'll be okay."

The words rang hollow in her ears, however. She wasn't at all sure if they would be okay. Walking to Burlington would not be easy, and she dared not move around at night. It was too exposed, and she'd be vulnerable to attack. "We'll go as far as we can, then look for a safe spot to camp for the night. Okay, boy?"

"Woof," Cooper answered, running a few steps ahead. He stopped and looked back, daring her to follow.

"Alright, alright. I'm coming." Squaring her shoulders, Nikki followed her friend.

Cooper set a brisk pace, and she was hard put to keep up but didn't complain. The time for weakness was over. It was the apocalypse, after all. Zombies roamed free, people were treacherous, and the world was a dangerous place.

She couldn't allow fear to hold her back. Not anymore. She had to face what was out there, and she had to live her life to the fullest. With determined strides, Nikki braved the road toward Burlington and her brother, one step at a time.

The End.

But there's a lot more where this came from. Turn the Tide, Book 6 in the series, is now available on Amazon, and I've included a sneak peek at some of my other works. Continue the adventure!

Available on Amazon -
https://www.amazon.com/dp/B0BVM6XKRD

Do you want more?

So we've reached the end of From the Ashes, and I hope you enjoyed reading the book as much as I enjoyed writing it. If you did, please consider leaving a review. It would be much appreciated.

But that's not all. The sequel, Turn the Tide, Book 6 in the series, is now available on Amazon, plus I've included a sneak peek below. Enjoy!

Turn the Tide
Prologue I - Nikki

Nikki set a steady pace toward Burlington, leaving the truck with its empty gas tank behind. While she didn't like being out in the open, she had no choice. Not if she wanted to reach the city in one piece and unzombified.

Cooper didn't share her reservations about walking. He loved running in the fresh air and disliked being stuck inside a vehicle for too long. Smiling at the dog, her new best friend, she said, "Come on, Cooper. Let's go."

As Nikki walked, her head kept moving from side to side, ever alert for danger. She knew she couldn't afford to let her guard down. Not even for a few seconds. She'd seen what the zombies could do, which was not pretty. They had a way of popping up in the unlikeliest of places, like a constant game of whack-a-mole, only deadlier.

At least she had Cooper to help watch for them. The dog had boundless energy and circled her constantly as they moved, his nose to the ground. His senses were much stronger than hers, and she trusted him to warn her of possible danger. Still, she couldn't rely solely on him. That would be a mistake.

As they walked, tall brush and scraggly trees lined either side of the road. It was the type of terrain she didn't like, making her feel hemmed in on all sides. Plus, the brush provided a million hiding spots for both the living and the dead, neither of which she trusted.

Chewing on her bottom lip with worry, Nikki picked up the pace. Hopefully, the terrain would clear up soon. She much preferred open farmland and fields.

As she walked, her mind wandered to the time before the outbreak. To a life spent under the heel of her abusive stepfather, Rex. She supposed that placed her in a unique position. Unlike most people, she didn't miss her former life. Not one bit. Nor did she miss Rex. Ultimately, he deserved what he got—becoming a zombie before dying at her hand. It was fate. Pure and simple.

Now, all that mattered was survival. She had to be vigilant, cautious, and smart. It was a chance at a new life for her, no matter how bloody or brutal, and she was intent on making the most of it. Picking up a random stick, she tossed it in the air. "Fetch, Cooper!"

Cooper obliged, barking and wagging his tail as he ran after the stick. She smiled as she watched him run back, eager for her to throw it again.

"Good boy," Nikki said, patting him on the head.

The brush thinned out as they continued their journey until

it mainly became trees. Their tall, spindly trunks reached to the clouds, and a thick carpet of dead leaves and pine needles covered the floor.

It allowed her to see further, and Nikki relaxed a little as time passed. Birds flitted overhead, their warbling cries echoing through the canopy. Coupled with the warm winter sun and fresh air, she could almost imagine being on a scenic hike.

Almost.

Suddenly, Cooper's ears perked up, and he growled low in his throat. His hackles rose as he focused on the road ahead.

Nikki's heart skipped a beat, and she reached for her gun. Staring ahead, she tried to see what Cooper saw, but it was impossible. The road curved to the left, the view obscured. Then she heard the sound of shuffling feet coming closer. It was a familiar sound. Unmistakable.

Zombies.

A lot of zombies.

Nikki wavered, trying to decide on a plan of action but realized she had none. She wasn't prepared for this. She hadn't even thought about what to do if a group of zombies appeared. One or two, maybe. Even three. That was what the gun on her hip was for, but a whole group?

The closest she had to a plan was running, which wasn't much of a plan. Her palms started to sweat as the first zombies came into view. More followed, and her stomach dropped. There were at least ten of them, moving fast, with blank stares and moans that set her teeth on edge.

Cooper barked, and Nikki knew it was time to go. She gripped the straps of her backpack with both hands and started to run. She headed off the road and straight into the forest, hoping to lose the infected between the trees. Cooper was right by her side, a golden bullet streaking across the forest floor.

The zombies spotted her and gave chase, their keening cries akin to the howling of wolves. They were the predators, and she was the prey.

Nikki's heart raced as she darted through the woods, her feet pounding the earth. The zombies were close behind, their hands outstretched. For corpses, they were surprisingly fast, especially when they were freshly turned, and they never tired. The same didn't apply to her. She could almost feel their breath on the back of her neck, making her skin crawl.

Fueled by adrenaline and the fear of death, Nikki pushed herself to run faster than ever. Her heart hammered as she dodged trees and jumped over deadfalls. Twigs slapped her in the face, branches tore at her clothes, and rocks rolled underfoot. She almost lost her balance a few times, her arms windmilling in the air, but she never gave up.

A glance over her shoulder showed her the distance between her and the pack of zombies had widened. She'd won a few precious minutes, but her energy was quickly running out. She had to lose the zombies before she ran out of steam.

Then she saw it- a large fallen tree trunk. It was hollowed out on one end, creating the perfect hiding spot. Nikki pointed to the tree and yelled to Cooper, "In there!"

Cooper bounded toward the opening and disappeared inside like a golden flash. Nikki followed, shrugging off her backpack before squeezing into the small space. Using her pack as a shield, she closed the gap with its canvas bulk. Stuck inside the dank, dark trunk, she held onto Cooper with one hand and her pack with the other. *Please, please, please let this work.*

She sat there for what felt like an eternity, listening as the zombies shambled past her hiding spot. They were so close she could hear their labored movements and the sound of their rotting flesh brushing against the tree trunks. The stench of decay was overpowering, and she fought against the urge to gag.

Cooper trembled against her side, and she prayed he wouldn't growl. Pulling him close, she held him tight. The sound of her heartbeat thudding in her eardrums became her whole world: that and the feel of Cooper's warm body pressed against hers.

Finally, after what seemed like hours, the zombies continued on their way, their moans fading into the distance. Nikki let out a shuddering breath, her body shaking with adrenaline.

"That was too close," Nikki muttered, her voice barely above a whisper.

Cooper licked her hand and whined, sensing the fear and relief that filled her mind. "Good, boy. There's a good boy."

Still, Nikki sat frozen, unable to move. She knew they couldn't stay there forever but needed a few moments to gather her wits and plan their next move.

Taking a deep breath, Nikki dropped her backpack and peeked out of the hole in the tree trunk. The coast was clear, and she crawled out of the opening. Cooper followed suit, stretching his legs and wagging his tail.

A quick look around reassured her they were alone, but the sun hung low on the horizon. Nightfall was the worst, the darkness providing the perfect cover for the zombies. They had to find shelter and fast. "Let's go, Cooper. We need to get to the road."

Nikki turned back the way they came, retracing her steps until they hit the highway. The bland gray asphalt stretched ahead like the road to hell, and for a moment, she wanted nothing more than to give up.

Her legs felt like jelly after the long day's walk and the zombie chase. Her nerves were shot, and her back was bowed beneath the weight of her backpack. She was hungry, thirsty, and tired, but giving up was not in her nature. She was too mean for that.

Heaving a sigh, Nikki said, "Come on, Cooper."

With grim determination, she placed one foot in front of the other. Cooper walked next to her, but he was also tired. It was evident in the way he walked with his head hanging low and his tail between his legs.

"Don't worry, boy. We'll find a place to spend the night."

The sun was setting when they spotted a farmhouse in the distance. With cautious hope, Nikki sneaked up to the place, her gun in her hands and her senses on high alert. "Shh, boy. Don't make a sound," she warned Cooper.

But as they neared the place, they saw that the farm had been abandoned for years. The house was old and decrepit, the roof caving in and the windows shattered. The front gate was rusted and hung off one hinge. It was the kind of place that gave her the creeps, but it was also the only shelter they would find that night.

"Stay close," she whispered to Cooper, keeping him close by her side. She approached the gate, which let out a loud screech as she pushed it open. Unease prickled at her skin as they walked toward the house, but she couldn't see anything in the shadows.

Nikki stepped onto the porch, and the wood creaked beneath her weight. The door was slightly ajar, and she pushed it open with the barrel of her gun. Inside, the air was thick and musty, and cobwebs covered everything. The furniture was old and moth-eaten, and the floorboards groaned beneath her feet.

"Lovely," she said, wrinkling her nose.

She went to the kitchen, finding nothing to eat and drink as she rummaged through the cabinets. The place was barren, and Nikki concluded that the previous occupants had left long ago. She headed upstairs, finding a bedroom with a bed that looked like it had seen better days. She sighed, but it was better than nothing. "I guess this will have to do, boy."

Cooper whined but wasted no time curling up on the bed and promptly fell asleep. While he took a quick nap, she checked the bathroom. The taps were bone dry, but she used the toilet anyway, covering the results with toilet paper from her stash.

Afterward, she joined Cooper on the bed, removing his water and food bowl from her bag. Filling one with water and the other with dry pellets, she placed it on the floor and watched while he gorged.

It reminded her of her own needs, and she quickly downed a bottle of water. Though lukewarm, the liquid felt like heaven to her parched tissues, and she groaned with pleasure. "Oh, that sure hit the spot."

Cooper looked at her, his muzzle dripping with water.

"You know. I'm not even hungry anymore," she said with a yawn, but she forced herself to eat a protein bar anyway, knowing her body needed the energy.

With the bedroom door locked tight, she unrolled her bedroll on the sagging mattress and curled up inside. Lifting the edge, she patted the space next to her. "Come on, boy. Time for bed."

Cooper crawled inside, and they snuggled up close. They were fast asleep within seconds, the world outside nothing but a distant dream.

Nikki woke up to the sound of the wind howling outside. For

a moment, she forgot where she was, her groggy mind struggling to make sense of the cold and unfamiliar surroundings. Then she remembered. She was in an abandoned farmhouse with Cooper.

Shivering, she climbed out of bed and stretched her limbs, trying to rub warmth into them. Her muscles protested, sore and stiff from the long hike the day before. Walking toward the window, she gazed through the frosted glass, her breath forming puffs of white mist.

To her relief, there were no zombies around, but the winter landscape was cold and dreary, with gray skies and barren trees stretching as far as the eye could see. It was the kind of day that made you want to crawl back under the covers and stay there until spring.

Nikki sighed and turned away from the window. It was time for her daily ablutions, and with no hot water in the taps, she did not look forward to it. Grabbing her backpack, she headed toward the bathroom. After using the toilet, she removed her clothes and cleaned her skin with sanitizing wipes.

Next, she brushed her teeth using a bottle of water, combed and tied her hair into a ponytail, and pulled on a clean set of underwear and socks. The rest of her outfit was the same as the day before, except for a thick sweater, a woolen beanie, and gloves. She pulled them on, grateful for the warmth they provided.

Cooper stirred next to her, stretching his legs and yawning. He looked up at her with tired eyes, tail thumping against the dusty floorboards. Nikki patted his head and said, "Morning, sleepyhead. Time for breakfast."

He perked up at the mention of food, and she quickly filled his bowls with dog pellets and water. While Cooper ate, she made a meal of peanut butter and cookies, washing it down with bottled water and orange juice.

The meal wasn't very satisfying, but it was better than nothing. With a loud burp, she packed away her things and prepared to leave the farmhouse. It was shaping to be a long day, and she wanted an early start.

"Come on, boy," she told Cooper, climbing to her feet. "Let's go."

The stairs creaked beneath her feet, each sounding like a gunshot in the gloomy atmosphere. She checked the kitchen cupboards one last time, hoping she'd missed something the night before, but there was nothing. "Sorry, boy. No caviar for us today."

Cooper yipped and ran to the front door, scratching at the rotten woodwork with his claws. He seemed pretty frantic, and she guessed he needed to pee.

"I'm coming, boy. Hold your horses," Nikki said, heading over. She took one last look at the desolate landscape outside before opening the door a crack.

An icy wind assaulted her with brutal force, nearly pushing her off her feet. She clung to the doorjamb, her fingers and toes turning numb within seconds.

Cooper bounded outside, and Nikki followed, closing the door behind her. She looked around, taking in the bleak landscape while Cooper sniffed around, searching for the perfect spot to do his business.

Suddenly, he let out a low growl, his eyes locked on a shape in the distance. Nikki tensed, her hand moving to the hilt of her knife. She strained her eyes, trying to determine what had caught the dog's attention.

Then, she saw it. A man stumbling through the field, his

movements erratic and uncoordinated. He was a zombie, his skin gray and mottled, and he wore a tattered pair of coveralls that flapped in the wind.

What bothered her was his size, clocking in at an easy six feet three inches and three hundred pounds. She immediately abandoned any idea of hand-to-hand combat and reached for her gun. She stepped back, aiming her gun at the man's forehead. But before she could fire, he charged with hands outstretched.

Nikki's heart leaped into her throat as she pulled the trigger, the loud crack of the gun echoing through the desolate fields. The zombie kept charging, unaffected by the bullet that missed its mark by a mile.

A spurt of terror nearly caused her undoing, her knees buckling with fright. The distance between her and the infected closed, and her vision narrowed until all she could see was its snarling face. Her mind screamed at her to run, but she knew it was too late. It was fight or die.

Letting out a slow breath, Nikki squeezed the trigger. The bullet shot through the air and punched into the infected's skull. It exploded like a ripe melon, sending a shower of bone fragments, blood, and brains into the air.

Nikki stood there, gun in hand, her eyes fixed on the body. She couldn't help but feel a twinge of sadness at the sight. *He used to be a man once. Someone with hopes and dreams. A family. Now, he's just a rotting shell.*

Finally, she said, "Come on, boy. Let's go before more zombies show up."

Nikki left the corpse behind and continued her journey with Cooper nearby. As she walked, worry churned in her gut. While Burlington wasn't that far away, the road was dangerous, and she was on foot. It could take days to reach their destination. *Nothing is certain anymore.*

As if he sensed her mood, Cooper licked her hand and whined. Looking down into his golden brown eyes, she smiled. "It's okay, boy. I'll be alright. It's just a touch of the blues."

Cooper whined again and pressed his warm body against her leg. Reassured, Nikki lifted her head and faced the road with renewed energy. No matter what lay ahead, they'd face it together.

End of Preview. Continue the adventure here: https://www.amazon.com/dp/B0BVM6XKRD

Apocalypse Z - Preview

Read further for a sneak peek at my series, Apocalypse Z, a thrilling zombie adventure that will have you reading way past your bedtime.

Apocalypse Z - The Complete Collection
https://www.amazon.com/dp/B07XKVD6NH

Chapter 1

The people of Springfield thronged the entrance of the shopping center, jostling for space as they fought their way inside. Angry shouts were overlaid by shrill screams and the cries of frightened children. The blare of car alarms filled the parking lot, and columns of black smoke rose against the skyline. A single ambulance pushed its way through the dense traffic, the first one she'd seen all day despite the bloodshed.

Dylan grabbed a free shopping cart and added her struggles to the rest of the crowd, trying to get inside the supermarket. Coming here was a huge risk, but she needed food and water, or she'd never survive the coming days.

Gritting her teeth, she shoved her way through a gap between two middle-aged women. They screeched at her like banshees, their hostility palpable in the chaotic atmosphere, but she ignored them like the clucking chickens they were.

With her eyes set straight ahead, Dylan continued to forge a path through the mass of bodies blocking her way. She couldn't afford to care about anyone else or back down from a fight. It was every man for himself now, and people were desperate to survive. Desperate enough to kill, maim, or steal if need be. *And I don't plan on becoming a victim.*

She avoided the fridges and headed straight for the water, cramming a case of plastic-wrapped bottles into the bottom of her cart. The canned aisle was next, and she focused her attention on protein and vegetables such as tuna, salmon, corn, peas, soups, and tomatoes. Among the dried goods, she found a few protein bars and packets of dried fruits and nuts.

It was a struggle. Every step of the way was a battle, and Dylan grew increasingly aware of the gun nestled against her hip and the crowbar clenched in her right hand. She hoped she wouldn't need either weapon, but that was becoming more unlikely with each passing second.

A toddler stared at her as she passed, its face swollen with tears while its young mother fought to get her hands on diapers and formula. Two men wrestled over a television, and she shook her head in wonder. What did any of that matter now? Three more were kicking another that lay prone on the floor, his head covered with his arms. Blood spattered their clothes, and they looked like savages.

Averting her gaze, Dylan ran through the last few aisles, grabbing anything useful she could get her hands on. Coffee, sugar, powdered milk, dried beans, rice, batteries, toilet paper, and vitamins.

Suddenly, a strange woman blocked her way, wielding a steak knife. Her eyes gleamed above nicotine-stained teeth, and her breath smelled of alcohol. "Give me your stuff. Now."

Dylan bared her teeth and growled. "Fuck off."

The woman waved the knife in front of her face. "I'm not telling you again, bitch. Give me your stuff."

"If you want it, take it," Dylan taunted.

The woman grabbed the cart with one hand and pulled, still waving her knife in the air. Gripping the crowbar with both hands, Dylan swung it at the woman's wrist. It connected with a loud crack, and the woman screamed as she dropped the knife from her nerveless fingers. Letting go of the cart, she scrambled backward while holding her injured limb. "You bitch! You broke my arm!"

"You asked for it. Now scram!" Dylan said with a threatening wave of her weapon. The woman ducked away and disappeared into the press of bodies to look for easier prey, though Dylan doubted she'd be able to do much damage with her broken wrist. With a satisfied grin, she resumed her search for supplies.

As she reached the end of the aisle, the sounds inside the store changed in tone and pitch. Terrified screams rose all around her, a chant taken up by all as it passed around from mouth to mouth. Dylan froze on the spot as she fought to make out the words. When she did, all the blood drained from her face, leaving her cold and numb.

"The dead!"

"They're coming!"

"Get inside!"

"Block the entrance!"

People stampeded away from the doors. They pushed their way deeper into the store to get away from the horror that approached from the outside. Dylan knew only too well what it was, and fear spurted through her veins at the thought.

Desperation fueled her actions, and she pulled back from the surging mass of bodies before she could be crushed or trampled underfoot. Using her shopping cart as a battering ram, Dylan forged a path to the back of the store where a familiar door awaited.

Staff Only.

It led toward the storage room and loading bay at the back of the store, as well as the manager's office, staff quarters, and bathrooms. She'd spent a few months during the last year working at the supermarket as a bagger. It was the reason she chose this place above all the others that were closer to home. The reason she carried her old keycard in her pocket, praying she wouldn't need it, but hoping it would still work if she did.

Dylan reached her destination and pulled up to the heavy iron door, usually locked to prevent easy access. With fumbling fingers, she pulled out her card and ran it through the slot. A negative beep sounded, and the red light shined. "No!"

Behind her, the screams were growing louder, and she frantically tried again, but to no avail. The store had become a death trap. The crush of panicking people grew worse, and she was pushed up against the door with her loaded cart pressed painfully into her midriff.

Gasping for breath, Dylan scanned the walls and ceiling for an escape. Any escape. Abandoning her supplies was better than dying for them. A few windows set high in the walls beckoned, as did the fire escape on the far side. Could she make it to any of them?

A shoulder rammed into her side, and Dylan hissed as her ribs exploded in red-hot agony. She almost lost her grip on the cart, but managed to hold on as she fell to the floor.

She looked up in time to see the nearest rack topple over with a ponderous groan. It crashed on top of her, and only the shopping cart prevented her from being crushed. Bottles of bleach and disinfectant burst on impact, and harsh fumes burned her nostrils.

Through tear-filled eyes, she gazed around in horror. Many had not been as lucky as her, and several people were trapped or injured. The rest of the store continued its rampage of terror, the crowd killing itself as it tried to escape the undead.

Even as she stared, jerky figures entered the store and sprinted toward the nearest victims. With guttural growls, they pounced on their prey, digging their teeth and nails into any open flesh they could reach. The coppery scent of blood filled the air, and the masses were whipped into a frenzy as death approached.

Pinned between the wall and her cart, Dylan was trapped. No amount of wriggling or pushing could get the rack to shift even an inch. Sitting in a puddle of bleach, she closed her eyes and tried to regain a semblance of calm. "There has to be a way out. There has to."

A low snarl caused her eyes to pop open, and she found herself looking at one of the infected. He was perched on top of the debris like a hungry wolf, his teeth bared in a threatening grimace. Black veins crisscrossed his pale skin. There was something primal about him, something so wild she knew there could be no reasoning with such a creature. He was no longer human.

With her heart pounding in her chest, she watched him sniff at the crushed bottles of cleaning supplies, wrinkling his nose at the sharp smell. An injured woman groaned, and he honed in on her with deadly intensity. Pouncing like a tiger, he tore into the helpless woman's throat, and her screams were lost in a gurgling fountain of blood.

Dylan pressed her hands to her lips to contain her screams, but the horror was too overwhelming. Not caring who or what heard her, she twisted around and slammed her fists against the door behind her. "Somebody help me! Please!"

Undiluted fear coursed through her veins like acid, and she kept yelling and banging until her throat grew raw. A snarl caused her to look back. The infected man prowled toward her on all fours, blood dripping from his chin.

Dylan twisted to the side, reaching for her gun. Her hand closed on the pistol grip, and she pulled it free from its holster. Breathing hard, she sought to still her trembling hands. *Remember your training. You didn't spend all those afternoons at the range for nothing.*

The infected paused, and his thigh muscles bunched, ready to leap. She took careful aim. He was so close. Too close. *It has to be the head. That's what the CDC said in their last broadcast.*

As she pulled the trigger, a silly thought occurred to her. *Why was it always the damn head?*

The bullet drilled a hole between the man's eyes, and he collapsed with half of his skull missing. The next moment, Dylan fell backward as the door behind her opened without warning. A set of familiar blue eyes gazed down into hers, and she gasped with surprise. "Ben? Ben Randall?"

"Dylan? Is that you?" he asked.

She nodded, pathetically grateful to see her old manager. He'd always been good to her, and she prayed he still liked her enough to help her. "It's me."

He grabbed her by the arms and hauled her to her feet. "Hurry. They're coming!"

Dylan glanced at the inside of the supermarket and blanched. Every infected inside the space was running toward them, drawn by the gunshot. Her eyes fell on her cart, and her lips compressed. "I'm not leaving my stuff."

Jamming the gun back into its holster, she grabbed the cart's handles and yanked it toward her. It rolled inside, and she slammed the door shut with a yell of defiance. An avalanche of crap had followed the cart, however, and the door caught on a bottle of laundry detergent. "Oh, shit."

Kicking at the bottle with her foot, Dylan tried to clear the way, but it was hooked on something and refused to budge. An infected woman reached the entrance and threw herself at it with a screech. Her hand thrust through the opening and reached for Dylan's face. She ripped out a clump of hair, and tears filled Dylan's eyes. More infected followed, howling like wolves.

Desperate to shut the door, Dylan grabbed the woman by the wrist and pushed. "Get out!"

The infected woman was as slippery as an eel, but Dylan refused to give up. Sharp pain lanced up her forearm as the woman attacked her exposed flesh, but she couldn't let go.

At the same time, Ben yanked the blockage away from the door and yelled. "Close it now!"

Dylan slammed it shut, and the lock clicked into place, sealing them inside the storage room. Silence fell, broken only by their harsh breathing. The infected beat on the door, but the steel was thick, and it only registered as dull thuds. They were safe. For the moment.

On wobbly legs, Dylan stumbled toward the nearest crate. She wiped the sweat and tears from her face. Everything smelled like bleach, and her clothes were soaked with the stuff. Her scalp burned where she was missing a hank of hair, and her limbs were stiff and bruised.

Despite this, Dylan managed a tremulous smile as she looked at her rescuer. "We made it. Now, we just have to get out of here."

Ben stared at her with a grim expression, his spectacles slightly askew on his face. Somehow, that detail bothered her more than anything else. She'd never seen him with so much as a hair out of place. He was always painfully neat and tidy. "I'm sorry, Dylan, but you're on your own."

The fluorescent light above their heads flickered, casting Ben's face into shadow for a second. She frowned, unable to comprehend his words. "What do you mean? Surely, it makes sense to stick together. At least until we get out of here."

As he shook his head, he pointed at her arms resting on her knees. "That zombie bit you, Dylan. You're not going anywhere."

She stared at him for a breathless moment before dropping her gaze. Her eyes fixed on the tender flesh of her forearm, the skin smooth and unbroken except for a few scratches caused by long fingernails…and a half-moon crescent that leaked tiny droplets of blood. She sucked in a deep breath. When had that happened? She'd never even noticed it during the struggle.

It was a small wound. Not deep enough to warrant a single stitch, but it was more than enough to kill her. To send the virus tumbling through her bloodstream and into her brain. The world around her faded away as Dylan faced the undeniable truth. "I'm infected."

End of preview. Loved what you saw? Get the book right here! https://www.amazon.com/dp/B09KPM3BFQ

Your FREE EBook is waiting!

If you'd like to learn more about my books, upcoming projects, new releases, cover reveals, and promotions, simply join my mailing list. Plus, you'll get an exclusive ebook absolutely FREE just for subscribing!

Yes, please. Sign me up!
https://www.subscribepage.com/i0d7r8

About the Author

WEBSITE: https://www.baileighhiggins.com

Printed in Great Britain
by Amazon